Samuel French Acting Edition

Eating Raoul

Book by
Paul Bartel
Adapted from his screenplay

Lyrics by
Boyd Graham

Music by
Jed Feuer

SAMUEL FRENCH

SAMUELFRENCH.COM   SAMUELFRENCH.CO.UK

FOR PRODUCTION ENQUIRIES

UNITED STATES AND CANADA
Info@SamuelFrench.com
1-866-598-8449

UNITED KINGDOM AND EUROPE
Plays@SamuelFrench.co.uk
020-7255-4302

Each title is subject to availability from Samuel French, depending upon
country of performance. Please be aware that *EATING RAOUL* may
not be licensed by Samuel French in your territory. Professional and
amateur producers should contact the nearest Samuel French office or
licensing partner to verify availability.

MUSIC USE NOTE

Licensees are solely responsible for obtaining formal written permission from copyright owners to use copyrighted music in the performance of this play and are strongly cautioned to do so. If no such permission is obtained by the licensee, then the licensee must use only original music that the licensee owns and controls. Licensees are solely responsible and liable for all music clearances and shall indemnify the copyright owners of the play(s) and their licensing agent, Samuel French, against any costs, expenses, losses and liabilities arising from the use of music by licensees. Please contact the appropriate music licensing authority in your territory for the rights to any incidental music.

IMPORTANT BILLING AND CREDIT REQUIREMENTS

If you have obtained performance rights to this title, please refer to your licensing agreement for important billing and credit requirements.

OPENING NIGHT May 13, 1992

UNION SQUARE THEATER
under the direction of Raymond L. Gaspard

Max Weitzenhoffer, Stewart F. Lane, Joan Cullman, Richard Norton
present

Eating Raoul
The musical

Book by
Paul Bartel

Music by
Jed Feuer

Lyrics by
Boyd Graham

based on the film "Eating Raoul" by Paul Bartel

with
Courtenay Collins   Eddie Korbich
Cindy Benson   Jonathan Brody   Lovette George   Lauren Goler-Kosarin
Allen Hidalgo   David Masenheimer   M.W. Reid   Susan Wood

and
Adrian Zmed as Raoul

Set Design by
Loren Sherman

Costume Design by
Franne Lee

Lighting Design by
Peggy Eisenhauer

Sound Design by
Peter J. Fitzgerald

Production Stage Manager
Alan Hall

Musical Director
Albert Ahronheim

Orchestrations
Joseph Gianono

Vocal Arrangements
Jed Feuer & Albert Ahronheim

General Manager
Laurel Ann Wilson

Press Representative
Keith Sherman Assoc.

Casting
Julie Hughes & Barry Moss, C.S.A.

Choreography by
Lynne Taylor-Corbett

Directed by
Toni Kotite

iv

CAST
(in order of speaking)

Mary Bland .... COURTENAY COLLINS
Paul Bland .... EDDIE KORBICH
Dr. Doberman .... M.W. REID
Mr. Kray .... JONATHAN BRODY
Mr. Leech .... DAVID MASENHEIMER
Cop .... LOVETTE GEORGE
Howard .... DAVID MASENHEIMER
Donna the Dominatrix .... CINDY BENSON
James .... JONATHAN BRODY
Bobby .... DAVID MASENHEIMER
Junior .... JONATHAN BRODY
Raoul .... ADRIAN ZMED
Inez (Raoulette) .... LOVETTE GEORGE
Gladys (Raoulette) .... SUSAN WOOD
Yolanda .... CINDY BENSON
Ginger .... M.W. REID

Tourists, Swingers, Etc. .... CINDY BENSON,
JONATHAN BRODY, LOVETTE GEORGE,
ALLEN HIDALGO, DAVID MASENHEIMER,
M.W. REID, SUSAN WOOD

UNDERSTUDIES
Understudies never substitute for listed players unless a specific announcement
for the appearance is made at the time of the performance.

For Paul Bland—DAVID MASENHEIMER; for Mary Bland—SUSAN WOOD; for Raoul
— ALLEN HIDALGO; for Donna — LAUREN GOLER-KOSARIN; for Ginger — JON-
ATHAN BRODY.

Swings: LAUREN GOLER-KOSARIN, ALLEN HIDALGO

v

PRODUCTION NOTES

(1) Just prior to all versions of the musical number "A Small Restaurant," a bell tone sounds. This produces laughter from the audience (even the first time) and builds each time thereafter.

(2) Because the Blands are irritated by the Swingers living next door, it's funny if every time they open their front door we hear loud party noises, quickly, just in and out.

(3) The most important sound effect is, of course, the "bop" sound of the frying pan hitting people on the head. In the New York production we had a wonderful reverberating "bonk" which we sampled by hitting a pot with a mallet.

(4) It's also important to have fun with Raoul's accent. Adrian Zmed, whom you can hear on the CD of the show, did a great job.

— Jed Feuer

MUSICAL NUMBERS

ACT I

Meet the Blands ....Chorus
A Small Restaurant............................. Paul & Mary
La La Land...Chorus
Swing, Swing, Swing ....Chorus
REPRISE: A Small Restaurant .... Paul & Mary
Happy Birthday Harry...............................The Boys
You Gotta Take Pains .... Donna & Her Boys
A Thought Occurs............................. Paul & Mary
Victim Update #1 ....Howard
Sexperts.. The Girls
Basketball ....Basketball Player
Empty Bed ....Junior
Victim Update #2 ....Chorus
Tool For You .... Raoul & The Raoulettes
REPRISE: A Thought Occurs .... Raoul, Paul & Mary
Think About Tomorrow............... Raoul, Paul & Mary

ACT II

Entr'acte Victim Update #3 ....Chorus
Hot Monkey Love................... Raoul & The Raoulettes
REPRISE: A Small Restaurant .... Paul & Mary
Momma Said................... Ginger, Paul, Mary & Raoul
Lovers In Love .... Raoul & Mary
Mary .... Paul
Victim Update #4 ....Chorus
Eating Raoul ....Raoul & Raoulettes & Chorus
Trio .... Raoul, Paul & Mary
REPRISE: Eating Raoul................................ Raoul
I've Got to Stop Him..................................... Paul
REPRISE: Swing, Swing, Swing [optional].......Donna,
                                    Mr. Leech & Chorus
One Last Bop .... Mary
Finale ....Chorus

CHARACTERS

The Characters in *Eating Raoul* may be cast in a great variety of ages and interpretations. It is recommended that several of the secondary parts be played by the same actors.

MARY BLAND – very pretty, unconsciously sexy in a naive sort of way.

PAUL BLAND – prematurely balding, somewhat overweight and hopelessly square but sincere, tenacious and lovable.

DR. DOBERMAN – an officious lecher.

MR. KRAY – fat and mean.

MR. LEECH – an oily, smooth-talking womanizer.

METER MAID – hip and bored with it all.

HOWARD – bad taste incarnate who thinks he's hip.

DONNA THE DOMINATRIX – a kinky little bundle of energy with a voice as big as all outdoors; at home a sweet young housewife and mother.

JAMES – always smiling, would say or do anything to make a sale.

BOBBY – an obsessive case of arrested adolescence.

JUNIOR – a rotund gourmand.

RAOUL – a sexy young Latino with a weakness for girls and a talent to match his gigantic ego.

(cont.)

THE RAOULETTES (Gladys and Inez) – two knockout, if sluttish, young chicas. All boobs, butt and tongue.

YOLANDA – a former star of a certain age. Heavy Latino accent.

GINGER – built like a football player but dresses like Ginger Rogers—and can dance like her too.

Tourists, Swingers, Stick-up Man, etc.

TIME & PLACE

Time: Late 1960s. Place: Los Angeles, CA.

EATING RAOUL

ACT I

Scene 1

[Music Cue #1: OVERTURE]

Late 60's. Los Angeles, CA.
It is recommended that the various settings in the play be indicated by projections or the sparsest possible scenery. The play begins with a chorus. The singers may be seen or unseen.

[Music Cue #1a: MEET THE BLANDS, Part 1]

CHORUS.
THERE HAVE BEEN MANY FAMOUS TEAMS
COUPLES INTENT ON ACHIEVING THEIR
    DREAMS
FROM CAIN AND ABEL TO PAT AND MIKE
LOMBARD AND GABLE, MAMIE AND IKE
NICK AND NORA, SCARLETT AND RHETT
SODOM AND GOMMORAH, FRANKIE AND
    ANNETTE

SOME HAD IT EASY, SOME WENT TO EXTREMES
BUT NOTHING EVER GOT IN THE WAY OF THEIR
    DREAMS
SACCO AND VANZETTI, BONNIE AND CLYDE
NELSON AND EDDIE, JECKEL AND HYDE
THERE'S STILL A FEW THAT YOU MAY HAVE
    MISSED
HERE'S A PAIR WHO TOPS THE LIST

[Music Cue #1b: MEET THE BLANDS, Part 2]

MEET MARY AND PAUL
THE NICEST OF PAIRS
QUIET UNASSUMING TYPES
WHO DON'T PUT ON AIRS
THEY LIVE DOWN THE HALL
OR MAYBE UPSTAIRS
AVERAGE SELF-RESPECTING FOLKS,
A COUPLE OF SQUARES
MARY AND PAUL,
TOGETHER THEY STAND
MARY AND PAUL BLAND

(A pair of twin beds in which are sleeping MARY and PAUL BLAND, our protagonists. THEY are wearing matched pajamas. THEY yawn and stretch. The MUSIC vamps under.)

MARY. Good Morning, Paul, dear.
PAUL. Good Morning, Mary, honey. Sleep well?
MARY. Like an Angel!

(THEY blow kisses at one another without actually touching. As the number continues, PAUL and MARY mime getting up, washing, brushing their hair ...)

CHORUS.
SHE'S SEXY AND CUTE
HE'S NOT BUT HE'S SMART
SHE'S A FABULOUS COOK
TO HIM WINE IS AN ART
THEY'RE BOTH RESOLUTE
THEY SAVE ALL THEIR PAY
HOPIN' THEY CAN OPEN UP
A RESTAURANT SOME DAY
MARY AND PAUL, STALWART THEY STAND

MARY AND PAUL BLAND

(As THEY mime eating breakfast, the MUSIC vamps under. PAUL is reading his newspaper.)

PAUL. Mary, honey, do you think he knew?
MARY. The President? Of course not. These are the sixties, Paul. The President of the United States doesn't lie.
CHORUS.
THEIR MARRIAGE IS CHASTE
PLATONICALLY BASED
THOUGH LOOKING AT HER FIGURE
IT MAY SEEM LIKE A WASTE
THEIR UNION IS BLESSED
WITH MUTUAL TRUST
THEY ONLY HUG AND KISS 'CAUSE THEY'RE
DISGUSTED BY LUST
PAUL. Well, today's the day. James will be here around eight with the pictures.
MARY. I hope this place he's found is really perfect for our restaurant.
PAUL. Now, if Mr. Kray gives me that raise ...
MARY. What do you mean, if? Paul, you've got to be firm! He promised you!
CHORUS.
MEET MARY AND PAUL
AS THEIR SAGA UNFOLDS
THEIR STORY'S QUITE UNIQUE
THOUGH THEY'RE AS COMMON AS COLDS
MARY AND PAUL
THEIR FUTURE IS PLANNED
MARY AND PAUL
MARY AND PAUL
MARY AND PAUL BLAND.
PAUL. Mary, honey, I don't mean to nag, but have you done anything about applying for that loan we talked about?

MARY. I've got an appointment at two o'clock to see Mr. Leech at the bank.

PAUL. With my raise and your loan ...

MARY. We'll be on our way!

[Music Cue #2: A SMALL RESTAURANT]

(BELL tone.)

MARY. *(Singing.)*
A SMALL RESTAURANT
ON A COUPLE OF ACRES
FAR FROM L.A.
WITH ITS MOVERS AND SHAKERS
WHERE I'M THE COOK
AND YOU'RE THE WAITER
   PAUL.
AND THE ONLY AFFAIRS FOLKS HAVE, WE
   CATER
   MARY.
A QUAINT LITTLE INN
WITH A FINE REPUTATION
NEAT AS A PIN
WHERE NICE FOLKS VACATION
   PAUL.
VINTAGE WINES AND GREAT DESSERTS
   MARY.
NEIGHBORS LIKE FRED AND ETHEL MERTZ
   PAUL.
A FRONT PORCH AND A FIREPLACE
MOUNTAIN AIR AND OPEN SPACE
WE'LL CARRY A MORTGAGE INSTEAD OF MACE
   PAUL and MARY.
THAT'S WHERE I WANT TO BE
   MARY.
WON'T IT BE GRAND
OUR OWN COUNTRY KITCHEN

PAUL.
WE'LL CALL IT CHEZ BLAND
THE NEIGHBORS WILL PITCH IN
   MARY.
HILLS AND DALES AND FIELDS OF CLOVER
   PAUL.
A CAR, A CAT, A DOG NAMED ROVER
   PAUL and MARY.
OUR HARD LUCK TIMES WILL ALL BE OVER
SOMEDAY
ALL WE WANT IS A SMALL RESTAURANT,
FAR, FAR AWAY

(As THEY waltz, each disappears behind a screen and
"quick-changes" into work clothes.)

   MARY and PAUL.
A PLACE WITH LOTS OF PEACE AND QUIET
   MARY.
WHERE YOU'RE ROBERT YOUNG
   PAUL.
AND YOU'RE JANE WYATT
   MARY and PAUL.
WE'LL SCRIMP AND SAVE SO WE CAN BUY IT
SOMEDAY
ALL WE WANT IS A SMALL RESTAURANT
FAR, FAR AWAY
   MARY. Oh, Paul, look at the time!
   PAUL. 'Bye, sweetie. Have a good day at the
hospital.
   MARY. Thanks, honey, you have a nice day at the
liquor store.

Scene 2

As PAUL and MARY leave, the scene shifts to the streets
of Los Angeles. VOICE OVERS of various radio

announcements overlap.

ANNOUNCER 1. Checking the Hollywood freeway, traffic is backed up all the way to the West Covina exit. Motorists are advised to avoid …
ANNOUNCER 2. Fourteen teenagers mowed down by machine gun fire in an apparently motiveless killing at Hollywood High School …
ANNOUNCER 3. … third stage smog alert throughout the day, with air quality rated unacceptable for human consumption …

(Images of fast food, porno movies, pool halls and pawn shops fill the stage. A CHORUS of hippies, meter maids, movie stars and other L.A. types enter and sing amidst the sounds of traffic and police SIRENS.)

[Music Cue #3: LA LA LAND]

CHORUS.
WELCOME TO THE LAND OF FRUITS AND NUTS
WELCOME TO A WORLD OF BOOBS AND BUTTS
EVERYONE YOU MEET IS FROM NEW YORK
JEWISH DELIS HERE SERVE SHRIMP AND PORK
IT'S A MARVELOUS MECCA OF SUN AND PLAY
THE CITY OF WONDER, L.A.
LA LA LA LA LA LA LA LA LA LA LA LAND

(The scene shifts to the Psychiatric Ward of the hospital where Mary works. SHE is talking with DR. DOBERMAN. The MUSIC vamps under.)

MARY. But Dr. Doberman, I have a very important meeting at the bank! Please, I'll make it up to you.
DR. DOBERMAN. Oh, yeah? Meet me in Dialysis after your shift?
MARY. Dr. Doberman, I'm a married woman!
DR. DOBERMAN. I guess you'd rather empty the

bedpans in the psycho ward.

MARY. The bedpans! But I'm a nutritionist!

DR. DOBERMAN. That's the deal, Nurse Bland. Take it or leave it.

MARY. But ...

CHORUS.
LA LA LA LA LA LA LA LA LA LA LA LA LA LAND

(The scene shifts to the interior of Kray's Discount Liquors, a shabby establishment with an enormous display of cheap wines. MR. KRAY, who sports a Hawaiian shirt and a large gut is confronting Paul from behind the counter. The MUSIC continues to vamp under.)

PAUL. Mr. Kray I deserve that raise. You promised...

KRAY. Aren't you the putz who ordered twelve cases of Chateau LaFite Rothchilde at two hundred dollars a bottle? And now you're asking for a raise?

PAUL. I was only trying to class up the store a bit. A fine meal deserves a fine wine ...

(A STICK-UP MAN enters brandishing a gun at Mr. Kray.)

STICK-UP MAN. Hey, Baby, you got some cash for me in that register?

(A GUN SHOT, indicated by a drum rim-shot, is heard. The STICK-UP MAN falls to the ground, dead. KRAY produces his 44 magnum from behind his counter.)

PAUL. Mr. Kray! You killed him! Shouldn't we ... call the police?

KRAY. The police! That's it, you're fired!

PAUL. But ...

KRAY. That's it, you're fired!
PAUL. But ...
CHORUS.
YOU DO UNTO OTHERS BEFORE THEY DO
SOMETHING AWFUL UNTO YOU
THERE'S ALWAYS SOMEONE ELSE YOU CAN
   STICK IT TO
IN LA LA LAND

(As PAUL leaves, dejectedly, the scene shifts to Mr. Leech's office at the bank. MR. LEECH is an outwardly respectable businessman in a suit.)

LEECH. I've been reviewing your loan application, Mrs. Bland. And I'd like to check out your ... collateral.
MARY. Mr. Leech, my husband and I have been banking here since 1960 ...
LEECH. Oh, I'm sure we can work something out. How about dinner at my place? I have a hot tub.

(MR. LEECH places his hand on Mary's backside. SHE gasps and moves away from him.)

MARY. Mr. Leech, please! I'm a married nutritionist!

(As the scene shifts back to the street and PAUL.)

CHORUS.
LOOK ON THE FREEWAYS AND YOU'LL SEE
PEOPLE LOST IN EXHAUST DRIVING
   RECKLESSLY
THERE'S VALET PARKING AT THE A AND P
IN LA LA LAND

(Enter a bored METERMAID.)

PAUL. Oh my God, my car's been stolen! It was parked right here.

METERMAID. Right here? What's your license number?
PAUL. IL6734.

(SHE hands him a slip of paper.)

PAUL. What's this?
METERMAID. A ticket, baby. This is a "No Parking Zone."
PAUL. Don't you understand? My CAR'S been STOLEN!
METERMAID. Un-huh. Let's see your Driver's License, sugar.
PAUL. *(Reaching for his wallet.)* Oh, no! My wallet! I've been pick-pocketed!
METERMAID. *(Writing out another ticket.)* Driving without a license, sweetheart?
PAUL. But …
CHORUS.
THOUSANDS ARRIVE EACH AND EVERY DAY
IT'S THE FABULOUS, WONDERFUL,
    MARVELOUS,
REMARKABLE, ASTONISHING CITY OF L.A.
LA LA LA LA LA LA LA LA LA LA LA LA LAND

Scene 3

It is the end of the day and the crowd has pushed MARY and PAUL all the way to their apartment building. THEY meet at the front door. THEY are now in the apartment building hallway, and THEY are accosted by a group of SWINGERS. PAUL is carrying two large brown bags. MARY is carrying a stack of mail and dry-cleaning.

PAUL. Home at last!

MARY. I hope your day was better than mine.

(The scenery [or projection] adjusts and THEY are now inside. THEY rush to the elevator which contains a tall BRUNETTE with big boobs and a big butt, and a short NERD.)

PAUL. Would you hold the elevator, please?

(PAUL and MARY enter the elevator and are taken aback by the couple.)

WOMAN. What floor?
MARY. Five, please.
WOMAN. (*Never stopping for a breath.*) Us, too. We never miss Harry's birthday orgy.
MAN. What a turn-on!

(The strange COUPLE begin to kiss and caress each other outrageously.)

MAN. How about you two? You like to swing?
PAUL. Certainly not!

(MARY and PAUL exit the elevator into the hallway outside their apartment. The hallway is filled with SWINGERS.)

[Music Cue #4: SWING, SWING, SWING]

CHORUS.
WE'RE KISSIN' WE'RE HUGGIN'
WE'RE DRINKIN', WE'RE DRUGGIN'
WE'RE CRUISIN', WE'RE CHOOSIN',
EVERYONE HERE WANTS TO SWING!

WE'RE RANTIN', WE'RE RAVIN'
WE'RE MASTER-AND-SLAVIN'

WE'RE BOOZIN', WE'RE BRUISIN'
EVERYONE HERE WANTS TO SWING

(MARY and PAUL push their way down the hall toward their apartment. THEY are approached by HOWARD SWINE, a typical swinger. HIS shirt is open to the navel and HE is wearing lots of chest jewelry and grey leather zip-up boots. You can smell the hairspray a mile away.)

HOWARD. Hey, what's the rush? The birthday orgy is just beginning. You friends of Harry's?
MARY. We're not part of this group of degenerates.
HOWARD. You mean you don't swing?
PAUL. Certainly not!
HOWARD. Well, maybe you don't but I bet she does!
PAUL. Excuse us, we *live here.*
CHORUS.
ALL OF US LIVE FOR JUST ONE THING
WE WANT TO SWING, SWING, SWING

Scene 4

PAUL and MARY enter their apartment. PAUL has trouble with the door.

PAUL. Honey, the door is sticking again.
MARY. I've called the landlord a thousand times about that door. God, those people in 5J never stop!
PAUL. That's because they're perverts, dear.
MARY. Why does he let all these swingers move in? They're practically taking over the building.
PAUL. Because they're transient, that's why. Always pairing up, switching off and moving out again. The landlord can raise the rent every five minutes.

MARY. Sexual liberation!

(MUSIC begins.)

PAUL. They are exactly the type of person we should refuse to serve in our restaurant.
MARY. I can't wait to get out of this terrible building and this awful town.
MARY and PAUL. Some day.

(BELL tone.)

[Music Cue #4a: A SMALL RESTAURANT - Reprise]

MARY. *(Sings.)*
A HIDEAWAY LODGE
OUT IN THE COUNTRY
    PAUL.
FAR FROM L.A.
WITH ITS URBAN EFFRONTERY
    MARY.
A PLACE WHERE YOU WON'T FIND GRAFFITI
    PAUL.
ALMADEN OR RIUNITE
    MARY and   PAUL.
WE'LL MAKE IT THERE, WON'T WE SWEETIE
SOMEDAY?
ALL WE WANT IS A SMALL RESTAURANT
FAR, FAR AWAY

(As the song ends, PAUL looks deeply into Mary's eyes.)

PAUL. Let's ... eat. I picked up a nice little Bordeaux to go with our Duck à l'orange.

(PAUL starts for the kitchen as MARY goes through the mail.)

MARY. Let's see ... Bill ... bill ... bill ... oh, no, they cancelled our Bank Americard. Bill ... bill ... here's something from our landlord. (*SHE opens the letter and reads it.*) They're raising our rent twenty percent, and it's retroactive!

PAUL. We'll figure out something, honey. We always do. I'm going to start dinner. James will be here before we know it.

(*HE exits into the kitchen. The DOORBELL rings.*)

MARY. My god, There's James already!

(*MARY pats her hair and opens the door. The LOUD PARTY is heard. HOWARD pushes past her into the apartment.*)

MARY. You're not James! What are you ...

HOWARD. So this is where they're keeping the prime meat.

MARY. Just where do you think you're going?

HOWARD. Come on over to Harry's and let's get it on, doll!

MARY. Get out of here before I call my ...

HOWARD. Aw, don't be like that! Under these fancy clothes I'm really a very sensitive guy. Kiss me, bitch!

MARY. Oh my God! Help! Paul, help!

HOWARD. You like it rough, huh?

(*HE forces himself on Mary. Her screams bring PAUL out of the kitchen carrying a frying pan.*)

MARY. Quick, Paul, Oh, my God ... Help! Help!

PAUL. Oh my god, Mary! Let go of her, you low-life sex maniac!

(HE struggles with HOWARD to no avail and finally bops him on the head with the frying pan. HOWARD, stunned, stumbles about the apartment a bit, before collapsing on the floor. As HE goes down HE rips one of the drapes from the window. MARY kneels down and feels Howard's pulse.)

MARY. Paul, you killed him! He's dead!
PAUL. What do you mean, dead?
MARY. Dead!
PAUL. Dead? Oh, no. What are we going to do? We gotta get him out of here.
MARY. Stay calm, just ... stay calm. We'll leave him out in the hall. Those people are so drunk they'll think he fell down the stairs. Let's hurry.

(THEY pick up Howard's corpse and start to carry it toward the front door. The DOORBELL rings. THEY panic.)

MARY. It's James! Quick, let's stick him in the closet.
PAUL. With my wine collection?!
MARY. Paul!

(MARY takes Howard's feet, PAUL takes his arms. But THEY go off in different directions and the corpse falls back on the floor. The DOORBELL rings again. THEY manage to stuff Howard into a closet but THEY have difficulty keeping the door shut.)

PAUL. Coming!
MARY. Coming ... coming.
PAUL. Just a minute.

(The DOORBELL rings again. PAUL and MARY try to gain their composure as THEY open the door. TWO MUSCLE MEN in lycra bikinis, black boots and dog

*collars rush past Mary and Paul. THEY are wearing
full face masks with zippers over the mouths. THEY
unzip. ONE takes out a pitch pipe and sounds a note
while the OTHER makes an announcement.)*

2ND BOY. We have a Singing Sadistogram for
Harry.

(THEY sing a cappella.)

[Music Cue #5: HAPPY BIRTHDAY, HARRY]

BOYS.
HAPPY BIRTHDAY HARRY
SIT DOWN AND SHUT UP
YOU'RE LOOKING SWELL FOR FIFTY
STILL FRISKY AS A PUP
IT'S YOUR BIRTHDAY HARRY
AND TONIGHT YOU'LL GET YOUR KICKS

'CAUSE THE GANG CHIPPED IN AND BOUGHT
    YOU A NIGHT
OF SADO-MASOCHISTIC DELIGHT
WITH THAT FABULOUS BUNDLE OF DONNAMITE
DONNA THE DOMINATRIX

*(One of the MUSCLE MEN opens the door. DONNA
enters. SHE is barely five feet tall in her stiletto heels
and wears full S&M regalia. Fishnets, garters,
bullwhip, the works.)*

DONNA. Many happy returns of the day, Harry.
PAUL. You're making a terrible mis ...
DONNA. *(Pushing Paul and cracking her whip.)*
Shut up ... tubby.
MARY. Just a minute ...
DONNA. Listen up!

(THE BOYS hold MARY back and tie PAUL to a chair.)

[Music Cue #6: YOU GOTTA TAKE PAINS]

DONNA.
WHEN BABY IS BAD
WATCH ME GET MAD
WATCH ME TURN RED
I'M LOSING MY HEAD
DONNA'S THE BOSS
SO DON'T MAKE ME CROSS
YOU GOT TO TAKE PAINS TO PLEASE DONNA

WHEN BABY IS BAD
WATCH ME GET MAD
WATCH ME GET HOT LIKE AN OVEN
IT'LL BE YOU I'M PUSHIN' AND SHOVIN' INTO
    THE DIRT
AND IT'S GONNA HURT

IF YOU SHOULD BE A BAD LITTLE BOY
I'M GONNA BREAK YOUR BEDTIME TOY
I'LL CARVE MY NAME IN YOUR BIG FAT TUSH
AND THEN I'LL LEND NEW MEANING TO THE
    BURNING BUSH
    BOYS.
SHE'S GONNA LEND NEW MEANING TO THE
    BURNING BUSH
WHEN BABY IS, BABY IS, BABY IS BAD
DONNA GETS, DONNA GETS, DONNA GETS MAD
YOU'RE BETTER OFF DEAD
'CAUSE IT'S JUST LIKE WE SAID
YOU GOT TO TAKE PAINS TO PLEASE DONNA
    DONNA.
I'LL STUFF EACH NOSTRIL WITH A CHAMPAGNE
    CORK
THEN REARRANGE YOUR FACE WITH A

COCKTAIL FORK
I'LL MAKE YOU SWALLOW A RED HOT COAL
THEN BEG FOR WATER FROM A DOGGY BOWL
   BOYS.
YOU'RE GONNA BEG FOR WATER FROM A
   DOGGY BOWL
   DONNA.
WHEN BABY IS BAD
WATCH ME GET MAD
WATCH ME GET HOT LIKE A PISTOL
YOU'RE GONNA FIND MY LITTLE FIST'LL
BE DOWN YOUR THROAT
   BOYS.
DON'T GET HER GOAT
   DONNA.
I'M GOING TO STRIP YOU DOWN
TO YOUR BVD'S
   BOYS.
YOU BETTER DROP DOWN ON YOUR KNEES
YOU SLEAZE
   ALL.
I HOPE WE'VE MADE IT CLEAR
IT'S NOT EASY TO PLEASE
DONNA! THE DOMINATRIX!

   PAUL. You're making a terrible mistake. I'm not Harry. Harry lives in 5J, this is 5G. You've got the wrong apartment.

(DONNA checks the door; loud PARTY NOISE in and out.)

   DONNA. What? 5-G ... Oh. (*To one of the Boys.*) Stupid. Go tell Lenny to hold the snake.
   BOY 1. (*Meekly.*) I'm sorry, Donna. I don't have my lenses in ...

(The TWO MEN exit. Loud PARTY NOISE in and out.)

DONNA. I know how you feel. It's like you opened someone else's mail. Mistakes happen, you know.

PAUL. Would you mind untying me?

DONNA. Sure. Look, here's my card. If there's ever anything I can ...

MARY. (*Indignant.*) It's extremely unlikely. Paul, please show ... (*Reading the card*) "Miss Dominatrix" to the door. James will be here any minute and we have that "duck" in the oven.

DONNA. I'm so embarrassed. Have a nice day! (*Yelling off to the Boys.*) You knuckleheads are in big trouble! (*SHE exits, loud PARTY NOISE in and out.*)

MARY. Can you believe that people actually pay money to be attacked with a whip? It's disgusting.

PAUL. A lot of swingers apparently enjoy that sort of thing. Mary ... what do you suppose makes them go for all that weird stuff? Are they crazy?

MARY. They're sick, Paul. This country is overflowing with millions of sex freaks.

PAUL. We're so lucky to have found each other.

(*Howard's BODY starts to slide out of the closet. PAUL quickly pushes it back in and closes the closet door.*)

PAUL. What are we going to do about him?

MARY. Don't panic. Shouldn't we call the police?

PAUL. Call the police, that's it. We'll call the police. After all, it was self defense.

MARY. (*Picks up the phone.*) Hello, operator? Give me the police ... yes, this is an emergency. Hello, police department? I want to report a murder ...

PAUL. Not a murder, an accidental death!

MARY. I'm sorry, an accidental death. My husband accidentally smashed this man's head in with a ...

PAUL. Hang up!

(*The DOORBELL rings. As if in response, Howard's BODY comes flopping out of the closet. MARY and*

PAUL panic.)

MARY. ... uh, never mind. Wrong number.

(SHE hangs up the phone. The DOORBELL rings. SHE crosses to the closet.)

PAUL. James!
MARY. You answer the door, I'll take care of ...
PAUL. But what will I say to James? What do real estate brokers talk about?

(As MARY shoves Howard's CORPSE back into the closet, PAUL opens the door. JAMES enters, a fast talker and a hard sell. PAUL tries unsuccessfully to hide the frying pan behind his back.)

JAMES. *(Seeing the skillet.)* How sweet! I see you're already practicing for your new career. Well, you'll be glad to know I'm starving.
PAUL. Oh, I'm afraid we had to cancel dinner. We had an accident ... in the kitchen.
JAMES. *(Taken aback.)* Oh, no. Maybe it's just as well. I have put on a little weight lately.

(PAUL just stares at James, unable to think of what to do or say.)

JAMES. And where's the lovely Mrs. Bland?
PAUL. She's, ah ... in the closet.
JAMES. Oh, yes?

(Pause.)

PAUL. Picking out something ... to wear. *(To Mary.)* Dear, James is here. Come out of the closet.

(MARY comes out, starts to walk towards James. The

BODY starts to fall out of the closet. PAUL runs over and leans against the closet door.)

MARY. How nice to see you, James.
JAMES. My pleasure. I'll only stay a sec. Paul told me about your little accident in the kitchen.
MARY. He did?!
JAMES. I just wanted to drop off these snapshots and a floor plan. This place is fabulous. Take a look. *(HE takes out photos, shows them to Mary.)*
MARY. Oh, it's lovely. Paul, you have to see this!

(Eager, PAUL starts to walk towards them. The BODY starts to fall out of the closet. HE can't leave. MARY realizes what's happening.)

MARY. I'll bring them to you. *(MARY crosses to Paul and shows him the photos.)*
JAMES. *(Unrolls the floor plan.)* The layout is ideal. Huge kitchen, you can put the dining room over ... Is the light better over there? Let me show you. *(HE crosses to where they are leaning again the closet door.)* Wouldn't you kill for a place like this? They're asking a hundred thousand, firm, and they want twenty thousand down. I know it's a lot but this place really is perfect, isn't it?
MARY. Perfect.
PAUL. Just ... perfect.

(Pause.)

JAMES. Well, think it over. Call me when you've made up your minds. This place won't be on the market long.
PAUL. Perfect.

(JAMES gives him an odd look and starts towards the door. MARY and PAUL both move to show him out. The BODY begins to fall out of the closet. MARY and

PAUL go back to hold it in. MARY motions to Paul to show James out.)

PAUL. (*Distracted.*) Thanks for coming, James.
JAMES. Oh, it was delicious. I mean ... it's my pleasure. I assume I'll be hearing from you soon?
PAUL. Sure, in eight to ten ...
MARY. ... days ...eight to ten days.

(JAMES exits.)

[Music Cue #7: WHAT A DAY!]

PAUL. Twenty thousand dollars. Wow! Well, when we get the money from the loan ... (*Reading Mary's face.*) ... no loan?
MARY. No loan. But don't worry Paul, I'll pick up extra shifts at the hospital. Did you ask Mr. Kray for the raise?... (*Reading Paul's face.*) ... no raise?
PAUL. No job. I was fired today.
MARY. Fired? Well, you can get another job and we can sell your car ... (*Reading Paul's face.*) ... Oh no, don't tell me you had an accident?
PAUL. Stolen, plus I got two parking tickets. And I was pick-pocketed.

(MUSIC note: the following is punctuated by diminished chords, chromatically rising.)

MARY. What a day!
PAUL. Fired, just like that.
MARY. Doctor Doberman attacked me.
PAUL. My car was stolen.
MARY. Mr. Leech at the bank attacked me.
PAUL. We didn't get our loan.
MARY. A drunk swinger attacked me.
PAUL. They raised our rent.
MARY. Cancelled our Bank Americard.

PAUL. No money in the bank.

MARY. And all we need is ...

PAUL and MARY. ... twenty thousand dollars!

PAUL. I know things look bleak, honey, but try to look on the bright side.

(The CORPSE falls out of the closet and sprawls on the floor at their feet. THEY both look at it.
End of MUSIC stings.)

MARY. God, I forgot all about him.

PAUL. Who is he anyway? Does he have any identification?

(MARY takes out his wallet and goes through it while PAUL sits on the sofa in a daze.)

MARY. (*Reading Howard's business card.*) Howard Swine, Jr. He's a Vice President of the Bank of San Fernando, Credit Division.

PAUL. He's probably the one who cancelled our Bank Americard.

MARY. Paul, there's over two hundred dollars in his wallet!

PAUL. Why do these swingers always seem to have so much money?

[Music Cue #8: A THOUGHT OCCURS]

MARY.
A THOUGHT OCCURS TO ME TONIGHT WE
    KILLED A MAN
BLIGHTS ON SOCIETY
BELONG IN A GARBAGE CAN
THE FILTHY PERVERT TRIED TO MUG AND RAPE
    ME
LOOK WHAT HE DID TO OUR RUG AND DRAP'RY
GO GET A HEFTY BAG

HIS GUY IS HUMAN TRASH
> **PAUL.**

I THINK I'M GONNA GAG
> **MARY.**

HIS WALLET'S FULL OF CASH
PAUL, IT'S ALL TAX FREE, IT'S HEAVEN SENT
WHAT A HAUL, WE'LL FIX THE TV, PAY THE
RENT
HAS IT OCCURRED TO YOU
THIS COULD BE QUITE A COUP
IF THIS HAPPENED EVERY DAY
WE COULD HAVE OUR RESTAURANT BY MAY
> **PAUL.**

MARY, WHAT ARE YOU THINKING?
MARY, MY STOMACH IS SINKING
> **MARY.**

COULDN'T BE MORE OPPORTUNE
SAY GOODBYE TO PAIN AND STRIFE
WE'LL BE SERVING DINNER SOON
> **PAUL.**

EITHER THAT OR SERVING LIFE
> **MARY.**

PAUL, OUR CASH FLOW HAS SLOWED DOWN TO
A TRICKLE
ALL OUR MONEY'S GONE, WE HAVEN'T A
NICKEL
YOU WILL HAVE TO LOOK FOR WORK
MESSENGER OR SODA JERK
WE CAN'T LIVE ON MY SMALL PAY
OR APOLOGIZE TO MR. KRAY

(PAUL thinks for a minute.)

> **PAUL.**

A THOUGHT OCCURS TO ME
YOU MAY BE MAKING SENSE
WE LURE THE PERVERTS HERE
THEN KILL IN SELF DEFENSE

I STILL FEEL QUEASY AND A TAD BIT NERVOUS
   MARY.
PAUL, THINK OF IT AS A PUBLIC SERVICE
   MARY and PAUL.
YOU AND I WILL SEE IT THROUGH
TOGETHER AS MAN AND WIFE
DOING WHAT WE HAVE TO DO
TO BEGIN OUR BRAND NEW LIFE
FATE HAS THROWN ANOTHER CURVE
WE'RE GONNA GET WHAT WE DESERVE
   MARY.
MURDER IS OUR ONLY CHOICE
   PAUL.
MARY, PLEASE, LOWER YOUR VOICE

(The MUSIC continues to vamp under:)

   PAUL. Mary, we wouldn't really ... I mean, you wouldn't actually ... you know ...

   MARY. Of course not! As soon as they try anything dirty, we'll bop them on the head like you just did and get rid of them.

   PAUL. But how will we find them? We don't know anything about this swinger stuff.

   MARY. *(Takes out the card that Donna the Dominatrix has given them.)* We'll just have to ask somebody who does.

   MARY and PAUL.
WE'LL GIVE IT A TRY
IT'S YOU AND I
IT'S DO OR DIE

Scene 5

The home of Donna the Dominatrix. SHE is now, in sharp contrast to her first appearance, the typical all-

*American housewife. As SHE speaks to MARY and
PAUL, SHE is feeding her 8-month-old BABY
(unseen in its cradle).*

DONNA. I think it's the cutest thing I ever heard.
(*Feeding the Baby.*) Come on, Jennifer, you like this!
(*To Paul.*) Are you going to work together?
PAUL. Oh, Miss Dominatrix ...
DONNA. Please, call me Donna.
PAUL. Donna, I don't think I ...
DONNA. Well, why not? That way you get the folks
that swing both ways. Those people have a lot of money,
believe me. (*To the Baby.*) Come on, Jenny, stop that
crying. Don't make Mama mad.
PAUL. God, whatever you do, don't make her mad!
MARY. Does your husband know about your ... ?
DONNA. Sure, I'm putting him through dental
school. This line of work pays a lot more than waiting
tables.
MARY. The thing is, we don't really know anything
about ...
DONNA. Listen, did you ever do any acting?
MARY. I was Laura in "The Glass Menagerie."
PAUL. In college. She was brilliant.
DONNA. Well, that's all it is, is acting. (*Lowering
her voice.*) Lick my sneakers, you little worm!
(*Resuming her normal voice.*) See what I mean? It's
easy!
MARY. (*Trying a commanding voice.*) Lick my
sneakers ...
DONNA. See, that was great! You're a natural.
(*Turning to Paul.*) Now, let's hear you.
PAUL. Oh no, I couldn't.
DONNA. (*Commanding.*) Come on. Try it!
PAUL. (*Awkwardly, with a very flat, monotone
delivery.*) On your knees, lady, and kiss my ... um ...
boxer shorts. (*Disappointed with his own performance.*) I
don't think I could actually say that to anybody.

DONNA. I know just how you feel. Everybody has his limits. For instance, I personally draw the line at Mashing the Yam. Listen, there's nothing to it! Just be sure to get the money up front. And whatever they ask you to do, stop if it draws blood.

PAUL. But how do we contact these people?

DONNA. Well, you could put an ad in the Swinger's Classified, or the Hollywood Sex Register. But if you really want to reach everybody, why don't you do a commercial on my TV show?

MARY and PAUL. (*Simultaneously.*) A commercial? What show?

DONNA. I do this talk show on Public Access T.V. KSEX, channel 14, midnight on Fridays and Saturdays. I'm like Johnny Carson, only dirty. You can say and do anything you want.

PAUL. What kind of people watch?

DONNA. You put a commercial on my show and I guarantee you'll reach every pervert and degenerate in Los Angeles County!

Scene 6

[Music Cue #9: VICTIM UPDATE #1]

HOWARD, the dead swinger, enters singing.

HOWARD.
NOW MARY AND PAUL
HAVE TAKEN MY DOUGH
AND BOUGHT THEM A SPOT
ON DONNA'S SHOW
IT'S TRUE THAT MISS "D"
HAS MANY A FAN
BUT SHE WON'T FOR LONG
IF THEY SUCCEED WITH THEIR LITTLE PLAN

IT'S MARY AND PAUL
IN X RATED LAND
IT'S ...

(BLACKOUT, LIGHTS up on LENNY, a seedy, low-life announcer.)

LENNY. Mary and Paul Bland, stand by. In 5 ... 4 ... 3 ... 2 ...

Scene 7

A T.V. screen on which is projected Donna's logo "Let's Talk Dirty," in black and white. We hear Donna's THEME. LIGHTS up on MARY and PAUL standing in place, with the TWO GIRLS they've hired to sing their jingle. MARY and PAUL are both dressed in full leather. MARY looks fabulous, PAUL looks silly. The THREE GIRLS are wearing black bars across their eyes and almost nothing else. The set and costumes, hair and make-up are done in shades of gray to simulate black and white T.V. A large "Sexperts" logo replaces Donna's logo.

[Music Cue #9A: THEME FROM
"LET'S TALK DIRTY!"]

LENNY. More of "Let's Talk Dirty" with Donna, America's favorite Dominatrix, after this word from our new sponsor, Sexperts.

[Music Cue #10: SEXPERTS]

THE GIRLS.
IF YOU'RE LOOKING TO SWING
COME ON AND GIVE US A RING

TWENTY FOUR HOURS A DAY
BE A SLAVE OR A KING
OUR STAFF WILL DO ANYTHING
KINKY, STRAIGHT, BI OR GAY

CALL SEXPERTS
FACILITIES FOR WHIPPING
SEXPERTS
FREE PARKING AND NO TIPPING
WE'RE SEXPERTS
CALL US TODAY

PAUL. (*Uncomfortable.*) That's right. Come down and live out your wildest sexual fantasies. We guarantee to live up to all your greatest "sexpectations." We got chains, we got hooks ... we got ... uh ...

MARY. (*Helping Paul out.*) We got handcuffs!

PAUL. We do B&D.

MARY. S and L ... I mean M!

PAUL. Sure we cost a little more, but we're worth it.

MARY. If you're not fully satisfied, your money will be cheerfully refunded.

PAUL. Cruel Carla, would you like to show our viewing audience one of our more popular routines?

MARY. Why, certainly. (*As Carla, surprisingly into it.*) Lick my sneakers you filthy worms. Cruel Carla's going to make you beg. And you better bring cash, no personal checks or credit cards.

PAUL. (*Taken aback at her sexiness*) Thank you, Carla! So, whether you're into bondage, or just want to chat, call Sexperts today. Dial 1-800-ORGASMS. (*The phone number 1-800-0RGASMS flashes*). Or drop us a line at P.O. Box 223A, Burbank, California. Take it away girls!

THE GIRLS.

SEXPERTS
WE'RE GONNA KNOCK YOUR SOCKS OFF
SEXPERTS
COME DOWN AND GET YOUR ROCKS OFF

SEXPERTS, CALL US TODAY.
 LENNY. Recommended by Swingers Classified and Mr. Big Magazine.
 THE GIRLS.
SEXPERTS.

BLACKOUT

Scene 8

During the BLACKOUT, we hear the OVERLAPPING VOICES of some of Paul and Mary's prospective clients.

 VOICE #1. Dear Cruel Carla: I pray I may have found in you somebody to help me over my fear of high-heeled shoes. If you would be willing to ...
 VOICE #2. Dear Cruel Carla: From you commercial, I can see you have the hands of a surgeon. There's this little operation I like to have performed from time to time and I will gladly pay ...
 VOICE #3 (Bobby R.). Dear Cruel Carla: You remind me of a very strict teacher I had in the the eighth grade. Enclosed is her picture. I would so love to relive some of those happy hours spent in the detention hall. Money is no object. If you could ...

(As BOBBY's voice cross fades with MARY's, the LIGHTS come up on Mary and Paul's apartment. PAUL, dressed entirely in black and wearing a face mask from the dime store, pushes on a flat painted to look like a church's stained glass window. MARY, dressed in a tight, black mini-dress, fishnet stockings and stiletto heels, finishes reading the letter.)

 MARY. ... keep me after school this Wednesday, I promise to behave and never disobey you again. Yours sincerely, Bobby R. (*SHE puts the letter down.*) Paul,

I'm a little nervous.

PAUL. Me too, but there's no backing out now. Remember, I'm right in the kitchen.

(The DOORBELL Rings.)

MARY. Just a minute!

(MARY finishes her outfit by tying a pair of rosary beads around her waist and placing an austere-looking wimple on her head. As PAUL ducks into the kitchen, MARY picks up a twelve-inch, surgical steel ruler. The DOORBELL rings again.)

MARY. Is that you, Bobby?
BOBBY. (*Offstage.*) Yes, Sister Carla. I'm sorry, Sister Carla.
MARY. Come in here right now, young man.

(BOBBY enters. HE is big and rather nervous. HE is wearing a parochial school uniform: shorts, white shirt and school tie. HE is carrying a school bag and a lunch box.)

BOBBY. I'm very late, aren't I, Sister?
MARY. Yes you are, Bobby. Did you bring your ... uh ... tuition?
BOBBY. Yes, Sister.

(BOBBY hands MARY a wad of bills. MARY stuffs them into her blouse.)

BOBBY. Are you going to teach me a good lesson?
MARY. (*Awkwardly.*) Yes, Bobby, Sister is going to teach you a *good* lesson.
BOBBY. Are you going to ... *spank* me?
MARY. (*Looking to see what is delaying Paul.*) Yes, I am ... going to ... spank you.

BOBBY. How hard?

MARY. (*Getting impatient for Paul.*) So hard ... you won't be able to sit down ... *ever*.

BOBBY. O.K., Sister, let me have it.

MARY. Bobby, Sister has to ... go to the principal's office for a minute. Why don't you take your seat and ... I'll be right back.

(*MARY goes to the kitchen where PAUL is standing right inside the door, his frying pan ready.*)

MARY. (*Whispering.*) What are you waiting for?

PAUL. (*Whispering.*) Can't you get him to do something to you? Touch you, anything? I can't hit him unless he makes me angry.

MARY. Paul, honestly!

(*MARY goes back into the living room where BOBBY is tearing open the pillows on the sofa.*)

BOBBY. (*Coyly.*) I've been bad.

MARY. (*Horrified.*) Oh my god, stop that! Stop that this instant!

BOBBY. (*Gets up and runs from Mary.*) Make me, Sister Bitch! (*BOBBY kicks his foot into the T.V. and knocks over a lamp.*)

MARY. (*As if being sexually aroused.*) Oh, Bobby, stop, stop, stop! No, no, not there! ... Oh god, I can't stand it ... oh Bobby, Bobby!!!

(*BOBBY stares at her as if she'd gone crazy. PAUL, meanwhile, rushes from the kitchen and bops him on the head with the frying pan. BOBBY falls to the floor.*)

PAUL. Are you alright? Where did he touch you?

MARY. He didn't touch me, he was destroying our

living room. (*Counts the money.*) Eighty dollars, barely enough to pay for the pillows.

PAUL. This may turn out to be harder than we thought.

MARY. It just goes to show you. You can read all the books in the world, but nothing prepares you for actual life.

(MARY drags the body into the bedroom as PAUL turns the flat around to reveal a basketball hoop.

The DOORBELL rings as MARY re-enters from the bedroom, now dressed as a cheerleader. PAUL tosses her two pom-poms and hides behind the flat. MARY opens the door and there is no one there. SHE looks to the right, SHE looks to the left and then SHE looks down to find a little man with glasses, wearing a black satin basketball uniform. HE struts into the room à la Super Fly. HE starts to sing, dance and scream à la James Brown.)

[Music Cue #12: BASKETBALL]

BASKETBALL PLAYER.
GO ON AND QUOTE YOUR PRICE
I GOT NO TIME TO QUIBBLE
SHAKE YOUR POM POMS GIRL
AND WATCH ME DRIBBLE
WHEN YOU CHEER REAL LOUD
I'M GONNA BLOW A GASKET
I WANNA DROP MY BALL INTO YOUR BASKET

(SCREAMS!)

WITH A CHICK LIKE YOU
I COULD PLAY FOR HOURS
BUT THE BEST PART COMES
WHEN WE HIT THE SHOWERS

*(The LITTLE FELLOW grabs Mary and starts to tear off
her blouse. PAUL's arm reaches around the edge of
the flat and bops the Basketball Player. BONK!!!!!!!!
HE collapses to the floor. PAUL immediately goes
through his wallet.)*

PAUL. Are you alright?
MARY. What an ordeal!
PAUL. Nobody can say we didn't earn this money.
(PAUL drags the body into the kitchen.)
MARY. How much did he have on him?
PAUL. (*Offstage.*) Sixty dollars.
MARY. I was hoping for more.
PAUL. Don't worry, we've got lots of others lined
up.

*(The DOORBELL rings again. JUNIOR, an immensely
rotund man pushes his way into the apartment.)*

[Music Cue #12: EMPTY BED]

JUNIOR.
I'VE GOT AN EMPTY BED,
BUT A FULL REFRIGERATAH
HELPS ME MAKE IT THROUGH THE NIGHT
KISS ME QUICK
YOU LUSCIOUS HOT TOMATAH
YOU LOOK GOOD ENOUGH TO BITE
I'M GONNA SINK MY TEETH RIGHT INTO YOUR
    BUNS
THEN I'LL SQUIRT WHIPPED CREAM ALL OVER
    YOUR ...

*(PAUL bops Junior on the head. HE collapses in a heap
and PAUL goes through his pockets.)*

PAUL. Are you alright?

(The DOORBELL starts ringing incessantly. PAUL and MARY try to drag JUNIOR'S body behind the sofa but THEY can't budge him. Angry and frustrated, PAUL finally abandons the struggle, grabs the frying pan, crosses to the front door and throws it open. HE is confronted by a six foot CHICKEN.)

CHICKEN. Cluck!

(PAUL bops him unceremoniously on the head and HE collapses in a heap on the floor, dropping the small package he was carrying.)

MARY. Paul, you just bopped the delivery man from Chicken Delight.

BLACKOUT

Scene 9

A CHORUS, consisting of BOBBY the SCHOOLBOY, the BASKETBALL PLAYER, JUNIOR and the CHICKEN, perform a crossover, singing cheerfully.

[Music Cue #13: VICTIM UPDATE #2]

CHORUS.
NOW MARY AND PAUL
HAVE BEEN AT IT FOR WEEKS
DEALING WITH PERVERTS,
GOOFBALLS AND GEEKS
THE HOURS ARE LONG
AND THE JOBS HAVE BEEN TOUGH
SURE THEY'RE MAKING MONEY
BUT IT ISN'T ENOUGH
MARY AND PAUL
WILL HAVE TO EXPAND

MARY AND PAUL ....

Scene 10

*The Bland's apartment. It's several weeks later and
    MARY is on the telephone with the grocery store.
    PAUL enters as MARY is speaking.*

MARY. Bland. B-L-A-N-D. 4252 South North
Street, right ... a quart of milk, a half of a pound of
butter, lightly salted, one hundred cases of Jello ... none
of your business ... strawberry ... and a pack of Juicy
Fruit gum. First thing tomorrow morning. Thank you.
(*SHE hangs up.*) Did you dump the bodies?
PAUL. All dumped. (*HE takes out the wallets and
starts to count the money.*)
MARY. Well, what did we make?
PAUL. All together ... about six hundred dollars.
MARY. That's all? Paul, we spent over three hundred
dollars on props and costumes! We'll never make the
down payment at this rate.
PAUL. It's not our fault, Mary. For some reason
we're getting stuck with middle-income sex-fiends.
MARY. Come on, honey, let's get some sleep.
Everything will be better tomorrow.

(*MARY and PAUL exit to the bedroom, turning out the
    LIGHTS as THEY go. For a moment there is silence
    and darkness.*
*The front door slowly opens and three shadowy
    FIGURES enter. The only light is from a
    FLASHLIGHT. THEY knock into the furniture and
    make quite a bit of noise. RAOUL stubs his toe.*)

RAOUL. (*In the dark.*) Gladys, you check the
jewelry. Inez, the silverware. (*RAOUL stubs his toe.*) Ay

chihuahua!

(HE discovers a box of costumes just as MARY and PAUL emerge from the bedroom. PAUL switches on the lights and RAOUL, GLADYS and INEZ are revealed. HE is a handsome Latino in his mid-twenties, dressed in skin tight black jeans and tee shirt. GLADYS and INEZ are two trampy Latino chicks. INEZ carries a radio and GLADYS a six-pack of Colt 45 Malt Liquor.)

MARY. You see, Paul, I told you I heard something.
PAUL. Who are you?

(RAOUL reacts as if Mary and Paul were intruders in his apartment.)

RAOUL. Wha ... Who are you?
MARY. We live here!
PAUL. This is our apartment.
MARY. Who are you?

[Music Cue #14: TOOL FOR YOU]

RAOUL.
I'M PLEASED TO MAKE YOUR ACQUAINTANCE
THEY SEND ME OVER FROM MAINTENANCE
I'M YOUR NEW SUPER
YOUR NEW SUPER ... INTENDANT
    MARY. It's midnight!
    RAOUL. I'm running a little behind with my repairs ... I do a gig at Yolanda's every Thursday night. Don't you recognize me? I am *Raoul,* and these are my *Raoulettes.*
    PAUL. You mean you're the janitor?
    RAOUL. Please! Superintendent!
(HE sings.)
YOUR T.V. SET IS ON THE BLINK

SOMETHING'S STUCK IN YOUR KITCHEN SINK
YOUR GARBAGE CAN STARTS TO STINK
YOU CAN CALL RAOUL

LADY, I'LL BE THERE IN A FLASH
TO SNAKE YOUR DRAIN OR DUMP YOUR TRASH
I GOT TIME IF YOU GOT CASH
LADY, CALL RAOUL

LET ME OIL ALL YOUR LOCKS
LET ME SEED YOUR WINDOW BOX
I GOT PLUNGERS, MOPS AND PAILS
MONKEY WRENCHES, NUTS AND NAILS
OR IF IT'S JUST A FUSE YOU BLEW
RAOUL'S GOT THE TOOL FOR YOU
    RAOULETTES.
RAOUL'S SO COOL
HE IS NO FOOL
AND HE'S GOT THE TOOL FOR YOU
    RAOUL.
IN TROUBLE, THERE'S NO NEED TO PANIC
JUST CALL UP YOUR FAVORITE HISPANIC
LET ME KNOW IF YOU'VE GOT A GRIPE
IF YOU NEED HEAT, BANG ON MY PIPE
I'M A HANDY MAN WITH A HANDY WIPE
LADY, CALL RAOUL

LET ME PLASTER UP YOUR CRACKS
I EVEN DO BIKINI WAX
I GOT PLIERS, PAINTS AND PLUGS
I'VE GOT STUFF TO CLEAN YOUR RUGS
OR IF YOU JUST NEED A SCREW
RAOUL'S GOT THE TOOL FOR YOU
    RAOULETTES.
RAOUL'S SO COOL
HE IS NO FOOL
AND HE'S GOT THE TOOL FOR YOU

RAOUL.
DAY OR NIGHTTIME YOU CAN CALL
I DO ODD JOBS, BIG OR SMALL
SO LADY DON'T YOU BE A FOOL
WHEN YOU WANT THAT SPECIAL TOOL
GO DOWN TO THE VESTIBULE
AND BUZZ B FOR BASEMENT
AND RAOUL
    RAOULETTES.
RAOUL'S SO COOL
HE IS NO FOOL
AND HE'S GOT THE TOOL FOR YOU

*(MARY has never seen anything like Raoul. SHE is
mesmerized by his gyrations. PAUL is annoyed.)*

MARY. Raoul ... Do you think you could fix the lock
on our front door?
    RAOUL. What? Oh, yeah. Sure, the front door.
    PAUL. Well then, fix it and please leave and next
time come at a decent hour.
    INEZ. *(Whining.)* Raoul, you promised you'd ...
    RAOUL. Inez, Gladys, you two go fix the leak in
4B. I'll be down in a minute.

*(INEZ and GLADYS exit. GLADYS flicks her tongue at
Paul on the way out.)*

    RAOUL. *(To Mary.)* You know you're a great
looking lady. How come you still live with your father?
    MARY. It's my husband. I mean, *he's* my husband.
    RAOUL. *(Notices the box of costumes.)* Hey,
what's all this ?
    MARY. Just some old clothes we're giving to the
church.

*(RAOUL picks up a red satin garter belt. PAUL grabs it
out of his hand.)*

RAOUL. What parish? St. Frederick's of Holly-wood? (*RAOUL knocks on the door with his mallet.*) There you are. Good as new.
MARY. So quick?
RAOUL. This door won't stick no more.

(*To demonstrate his handiwork, RAOUL opens the front door and slams it. The closet door flies open and a BODY, dressed as a SNOWMAN falls out on the floor.*)

RAOUL. (*Jumping back.*) Madre mia!!!!! Maybe you should explain what Frosty's doing here.
PAUL. We didn't kill anybody, if that's what you're thinking.
RAOUL. Who didn't you kill?
MARY. Any of them. The sex perverts.
RAOUL. Wait a minute, now I recognize you. Public Access. You're Cruel Carla. I saw your commercial. Wow, I can't believe it. I'm actually meeting Cruel Carla herself, in the flesh.
PAUL. And Mister Carla!
RAOUL. (*Looking at the body.*) Who is this guy?
PAUL. None of your business.
RAOUL. I bet the police would like to know.
MARY. He's a client.
RAOUL. I guess when your ad says you knock 'em dead, you aren't fooling. Cruel Carla, I can't believe it.
PAUL. What are you going to do?
RAOUL. I gotta hand it to you, you got a very original scam going here.
PAUL. (*Proudly.*) It was Mary's idea mostly.
MARY. Paul's just being modest ...
RAOUL. It would be a crime to turn you two over to the police ...
MARY and PAUL. What!

[Music Cue #15: A THOUGHT OCCURS - Reprise]

RAOUL. (*Sings.*)
A THOUGHT OCCURS TO ME
SUPPOSE I JOIN YOUR SCAM
OH WHAT A HELP I'D BE
THE BUSINESS MAN I AM
YOU KEEP THE MONEY
I'LL TAKE THE REST
LET'S START WITH THIS ONE
IT WILL BE A SMALL TEST

DON'T DUMP BODIES IN THE TRASH
THEY CAN BRING IN COLD HARD CASH
HOW DOES FIFTY-FIFTY FEEL
COME ON WHAT DO YOU SAY, A DEAL?
    MARY. A deal.
    PAUL. (*Taking Mary aside.*) Excuse us.
MARY, WHAT ARE YOU DOING?
MARY, TROUBLE IS BREWING
    MARY. (*To Paul.*)
HAS IT OCCURRED TO YOU
THERE WOULD BE NO MUSS OR FUSS
WHAT DO YOU SUGGEST WE DO?
HE'S BETTER AT THIS THAN US

WE'LL GET EVERYTHING WE WANT
REMEMBER THE RESTAURANT
COME ON, PAUL, WHAT DO YOU SAY?
    PAUL. Absolutely not.

(*PAUL won't budge. The MUSIC changes as MARY tries a new approach.*)

[Music Cue #15a: THINK ABOUT TOMORROW]

MARY.
THINK ABOUT TOMORROW

WHAT OUR LIFE COULD BE
THINK ABOUT TOMORROW
AND OUR QUAINT LITTLE INN BY THE SEA
    RAOUL.
THINK ABOUT TOMORROW
WHEN WE'RE ON OUR FEET
I'M ON A BILL WITH CHARO
AND THE TWO OF YOU ARE SITTING
IN A FRONT ROW SEAT
    MARY and RAOUL.
THINK ABOUT TOMORROW
WHEN WE'RE FREE AT LAST
MISERY AND SORROW
FINALLY HAVE BECOME
A THING OF THE PAST
    RAOUL.
THREE HEADS ARE ALWAYS BETTER THAN TWO
    MARY.
PAUL, PLEASE THINK THIS THROUGH
    MARY and RAOUL.
ALL WE'RE ASKING YOU TO DO IS
THINK ABOUT TOMORROW
THINK ABOUT SUCCESS
THINK ABOUT TOMORROW
    PAUL. My answer is ... No.
    MARY.
WE'RE GONNA NEED LOTS OF KITCHEN
    SUPPLIES
MACHINES THAT MIX AND OSTERIZE
    RAOUL.
WAIT TILL YOU SEE THE CLOTHES I'LL BE
    WEARIN'
SERGIO VALENTE AND CHAMPS DU BARON
    MARY.
WE'LL HAVE A MENU
FIT FOR A ROCKEFELLER
PURSUE THIS VENUE
YOU'LL HAVE YOUR NEW WINE CELLAR

RAOUL.
TAKE MY PROPOSAL
AND LET THE SCAM BEGIN
WITH ME AT YOUR DISPOSAL
WATCH THE DOUGH START ROLLIN' IN.
    PAUL.
I NEED TIME TO THINK
I'M NOT SURE I LIKE THE STINK
AM I WRONG OR AM I RIGHT
LOOKING DOWN THE TUNNEL
I DON'T SEE A LIGHT

IF I DON'T SAY YES
THE GUY STILL HAS OUR ADDRESS
AND OUR FUTURE SURELY BRINGS
THE NEED FOR A LOT OF EXPENSIVE THINGS

THREE HEADS ARE OFTEN BETTER IT'S TRUE
BUT WHEN THE THIRD HEAD IS YOU
IT MAKES ME WONDER WHAT TO DO
SO I

THINK ABOUT TOMORROW
AND IT SURE LOOKS GRIM
ESPECIALLY IF TOMORROW'S SPENT WITH HIM!

*(THEY sing a trio of the previous lyrics. The song builds
    to a climax interrupted by the TELEPHONE. PAUL
    answers it.)*

PAUL. Hello. No, we're still up. It's James. There
is? They did? We must? (*HE covers the mouth piece.*)
There's been another offer on our restaurant. We have to
let him know right now. Yes or no.
    MARY and RAOUL.
THINK ABOUT TOMORROW
PAUL, WHAT DO YOU SAY
THINK ABOUT TOMORROW

PAUL. (*Into the telephone.*) Okay. (*HE hangs up.*)
ALL.
THINK ABOUT TOMORROW
WE'RE GOING TO MAKE IT PAY
THINK ABOUT TOMORROW
PRIVATE ENTERPRISE
IS THE AMERICAN WAY

CURTAIN

[Music Cue #16: ENTR'ACTE]

ACT II

Scene 1

*A crossover by an assortment of Paul and Mary's victims
from Act I.*

[Music Cue #16a: VICTIM UPDATE #3]

CHORUS.
NOW MARY AND PAUL
ARE WELL ON THEIR WAY
BUSINESS IS BOOMING
IT'S BETTER EACH DAY
SINCE RAOUL ARRIVED
THEIR PROFITS INCREASED
AND HALF THE CITY'S PERVERTS
ARE AMONG THE DECEASED
MARY AND PAUL
ARE QUITE IN DEMAND
MARY AND (*SFX: Bonk.*)

*(The song is punctuated by a loud off-stage BONK! The
scene shifts to ...)*

Scene 2

*Paul and Mary's apartment. A table has been set up
behind the couch on which sit several telephones. On
each wall hangs a large Nazi flag. The couch is
decorated with little swastika pillows. PAUL has just
bopped HITLER. MARY collapses onto the sofa. Both
PAUL and MARY are sporting little Hitler*

moustaches.

MARY. God, I thought he'd never stop saluting!

PAUL. Mary, honey, would you mid bagging Adolph? I want to get set up for our three o'clock.

MARY. Oh, Paul, I bagged Tarzan and the Gladiator. It's your turn to ...

PAUL. (*Starts pulling down the Nazi banners.*) Well, I bagged the Gorilla, the Astronaut and President Johnson. Never mind, I'll take care of Adolph tomorrow.

(The TELEPHONE rings. MARY answers it.)

MARY. Sexperts. One moment. (*Putting her hand over the receiver.*) Paul? What's a hermaphrodite? Can we supply one?

PAUL. I'll check with the pet store, but I think they're expensive.

(The TELEPHONE rings again.)

MARY. (*Into the phone.*) Hello, Sexperts ... Let me check. Paul, do we have 220 wiring?

PAUL. You'll have to ask Raoul.

(The TELEPHONE rings.)

PAUL. (*Into phone.*) Sexperts.

MARY. Raoul. Gosh, look at the time. We promised to go see his act at Yolanda's.

PAUL. Do we have to?

MARY. Paul, we promised.

(THEY exit.)

Scene 3

[Music Cue #17: YOLANDA'S]

The scene changes to Yolanda's, a tacky Latino nightclub. There is a mirrored disco ball hanging from the ceiling and an exposed radiator on the stage, which is surrounded by a sea of empty tables. Downstage right is a table for two, marked reserved. YOLANDA, the owner of the club, a large Latino lady with flaming red hair, appears in a spotlight on the stage.

YOLANDA. Muchachas y muchachos, El Club Yolanda (that's me, Yolanda) is proud to present a new singing sensation. The hot, the sexy, the mucho macho sounds of the fabulous Raoul y Las Raoulettes.

(The MUSIC begins as RAOUL and the RAOULETTES enter, wearing jungle outfits. MARY and PAUL enter and are ushered to their seats by YOLANDA herself, THEY are seated just as RAOUL and the RAOULETTES begin to perform.)

[Music Cue #17a: HOT MONKEY LOVE]

GLADYS.
I DON'T WANT DINNER
I DON'T WANT DRINKS
AND I DON'T CARE WHAT MY MOMMA THINKS
   INEZ.
WHAT I WANT YOU GOT PLENTY OF
GIMME, GIMME, GIMME
HOT MONKEY LOVE
   GLADYS and INEZ.
SKIP THE FLOWERS
FORGET THE WALK
NO CONVERSATION
DON'T EVEN TALK

WE'LL FIGHT IF WE HAVE TO
WE'LL PUSH AND SHOVE
JUST GIMME, GIMME, GIMME
HOT MONKEY LOVE

GIMME, GIMME, GIMME
GIMME, GIMME, GIMME
HOT MONKEY LOVE

GIMME, GIMME, GIMME
GIMME, GIMME, GIMME
HOT MONKEY LOVE
   RAOUL.
I'M AT YOUR SERVICE
SO LET'S INDULGE
I'M GONNA MAKE YOUR EYEBALLS BULGE
I WANT THE SEX
DIRTY DREAMS ARE MADE OF
I'M GONNA GIVE IT TO YOU
HOT MONKEY LOVE
   GLADYS and INEZ.
GIMME, GIMME, GIMME
GIMME, GIMME, GIMME
HOT MONKEY LOVE

GIMME, GIMME, GIMME
GIMME, GIMME, GIMME
HOT MONKEY LOVE
   RAOUL.
I'M A SEX JUNKIE
SO MAKE IT REAL FUNKY
AND GIVE ME HOT MONKEY LOVE

YOUR BODY GETS HOT
YOUR LEGS TURN TO SPAGHETTI
YOU'RE GONNA MOAN AND GROAN
AND YOU'RE GONNA GET SWEATY

YOU'RE GONNA WRITHE
OUR HEADS'LL BE REELING
  ALL THREE.
THEY'LL BE PEELING US OFF OF THE CEILING
  RAOUL.
SO LOVELY LADIES
HAVE NO FEAR
YOU'LL BE GRINNIN'
FROM EAR TO EAR
YOU'LL BE SWINGING FROM THE CHANDELIER
  ALL THREE.
GIMME, GIMME, GIMME
GIMME, GIMME, GIMME...

I'M A SEX JUNKIE
SO MAKE IT REAL FUNKY
AND GIMME
HOT
MONKEY
LOVE

(THEY take their bows. RAOUL goes over to Mary and Paul's table.)

[Music Cue #17b: YOLANDA's]

RAOUL. Well, what did you think?
PAUL. (*Uninterested.*) Very nice.
MARY. You were fabulous.
PAUL. That's quite an outfit. Is it new?
RAOUL. Yeah, do you like it? It's a "yump" suit.
PAUL. I bet it cost a lot.
RAOUL. Plenty.

(INEZ and GLADYS come over to the table. GLADYS flicks her tongue at Paul.)

INEZ. (*Whining.*) Raoul, we need dinero for the

ladies room.

RAOUL. (*Hands the Girls a roll of bills.*) N o problem! Here you go, some for Inez, some for Gladys.

(*THEY take the money and exit, INEZ fanning herself with the bills and GLADYS flicking her tongue at Paul.*)

PAUL. Where did you get all that money?

MARY. (*Embarrassed.*) Paul!

RAOUL. Oh ... my Aunt Rosa died ... very suddenly. She left me a few bucks. (*Changing the subject.*) Hey, you two should stick around. This place gets hot in an hour.

PAUL. No, thank you. We have a big night ahead of us. Our biggest client yet. He's paying top dollar and he's booked three hours. Don't forget, you're due at our place at three a.m.

RAOUL. Three A.M.? Dios mio!

MARY. I really loved your show.

PAUL. Come on, Mary. Let's go.

MARY. 'Bye Raoul, see you later.

RAOUL. Ciao, Cruel Carla.

(*PACO, a rough-looking Chicano enters as PAUL and MARY exit. Watching Mary's retreating rear end, both Latinos grab their crotches in a macho gesture.*)

PACO. (*Drooling after Mary.*) Hey, nice looking goods.

RAOUL. Relax, Paco, I'm saving her for myself. You'll have to make do with the bodies.

PACO. Very funny. The dog food factory want to know when they can expect the next shipment.

RAOUL. Tomorrow. Now listen, I got a few more cars for you. A Buick Electra, a GTO and a Chevy Impala.

PACO. I'll take all you can give me.

RAOUL. There's going to be plenty more. Come into my dressing room.

(RAOUL and PACO exit through a door marked kitchen.)

Scene 4

The scene shifts to Paul and Mary's apartment. MARY and PAUL enter.

MARY. Wasn't Raoul wonderful?

PAUL. I don't trust him.

MARY. Why? Things are so much easier since we took him on.

PAUL. I want to know how he makes so much money with the bodies.

MARY. Who cares, as long as we don't have to worry about it.

PAUL. Have you seen all his new recording equipment? And how about all those tacky clothes he's been buying?

MARY. Paul, you don't think Raoul is cheating us?

PAUL. There's something going on. And I'm going to find out what it is.

MARY. Paul, honey, don't start anything. You mustn't lose sight of our goal.

[Music Cue #18:A SMALL RESTAURANT - Reprise 2]

(BELL tone.)

MARY.
A SMALL RESTAURANT
SURROUNDED BY FLOWERS
WHERE PEOPLE TAKE WALKS
AND NOT GOLDEN SHOWERS

PAUL.
FAR FROM POT AND SMACK AND COKE
  MARY.
WHERE HAM IS ALL THAT PEOPLE SMOKE
  MARY and PAUL.
WHERE WE CAN DO WHAT NORMAL FOLK DO
  EACH DAY
ALL WE WANT IS A SMALL RESTAURANT
FAR, FAR AWAY
  MARY. Come on, honey, we have to get ready.

(MARY exits. The DOORBELL rings. PAUL answers the door and it's RAOUL, who is standing there with two garment bags.)

  RAOUL. Hey, man, it's a quarter to three. Come on, you got to get dressed.
  PAUL. I'll be ready in a minute. You wait in the hall.

(PAUL closes the door in Raoul's face as MARY enters from the bedroom. SHE is dressed in a thirties "Ginger Rogers" ball gown and blonde wig.)

  MARY. Who was that?
  PAUL. Who do you think? You look great! What time is Fred Astaire due?
  MARY. Any second.
  PAUL. Good luck. I hope he brings plenty of cash.

(HE exits. MARY draws a glitter drape that has been set up across the back wall. The DOORBELL rings.
MARY goes to the door and opens it. There stands a large MAN, wearing an identical Ginger Rogers dress and blonde wig.)

  GINGER. If you paid less than I did for this dress, I'm just going to kill myself. Where's Fred?
  MARY. Fred? I thought you were supposed to be

Fred.

GINGER. No, no, you were supposed to be Fred. I'm always Ginger on these occasions. Go on now, change into your tux.

MARY. I'm afraid that's not possible on such short notice.

GINGER. Money? Is that the problem? I'll pay whatever it costs. Mama gives me a huge allowance, as long as I don't, you know ...

MARY. What?

GINGER. Hang around with girls who like to, you know ...

MARY. Smoke?

GINGER. No ...

MARY. Drink?

GINGER. No ...

MARY. What? What?

GINGER. Dance!!!

[Music Cue #19: MOMMA SAID]

GINGER.
MAMA SAID THAT GIRLS WHO DANCE
WERE EASY, SLEAZY
MAMA SAID THAT GIRLS WHO DANCE
WERE ALL WHORES

WHEN MAMA SPOKE I BROKE A SWEAT
AND GOT WHEEZY, QUEASY
MAMA SUFFERED EXTREME DURESS
WHEN SHE FOUND ME IN HER WEDDING DRESS

MAMA SAID THAT BOYS WHO DANCE
WERE SISSY, PRISSY
SHE LOCKED ME IN THE HOUSE
AND GAVE ME WHAT FOR

MAMA SAID THAT I WAS

REALLY A SINNER, NO DINNER
IF I TAPPED LIKE GENE OR FRED
I GOT KNOCKED UPSIDE MY HEAD
    MARY. Listen, this is a little more than I bargained for ...
    GINGER.
TODAY
MAMA'S IN A NURSING HOME
LEAVING ME OUT FREE TO ROAM
I SAW YOUR AD, LORD, WAS I GLAD
OKAY
TIME TO LIVE MY FANTASY
HERE'S YOUR CASH, NOW DANCE WITH ME
    MARY. No!
    GINGER.
DON'T GET ME MAD
I NEED IT BAD
IF WE DON'T DO WHAT FRED AND GINGER DO
LOOKS LIKE I WILL HAVE TO INJURE YOU
CUT THE CRAP, MISS THING, LET'S TAP!

(THEY go into an elaborate tap routine.)

    GINGER. Here's the part where the room breaks apart and the entire chorus of two hundred comes tapping down a giant, glittering staircase in white tie and tails!
    MARY. You're crazy!
    GINGER. I knoooooow ...

(PAUL and RAOUL enter, dancing, through the glitter curtain. THEY are dressed in white tie and tails and are carrying inflatable sex dolls, each dressed like Ginger Rogers.)

    PAUL, MARY and RAOUL.
HIS MOTHER SAID THAT GIRLS WHO DANCE
WERE EASY, SLEAZY
HIS MOTHER SAID THAT GIRLS WHO DANCE

WERE ALL WHORES
HIS MOTHER SAID THAT BOYS WHO DANCE
WERE SISSY, PRISSY
IF HE DARED TO TAP HIS TOES
HE GOT HIT WITH A RUBBER HOSE
  GINGER.
HURRAY!
HERE I AM IN TINSEL TOWN
IN MY TAPS AND FANCY GOWN
WHOEVER THOUGHT
DREAMS COULD BE BOUGHT?

(THEY tap to a big finish with PAUL producing the frying pan from it's hiding place on the sofa and bopping GINGER on the last beat.)

MARY. That guy was seriously disturbed.
RAOUL. Don't worry, he'll never tap at anybody no more.
PAUL. This was the hardest one yet.
RAOUL. And the biggest. We're going to need a lawn and leaf bag for this guy.
MARY. Paul, we're all out of garbage bags.
PAUL. I'll run down to the Mayfair Market and get some.
RAOUL. That Mayfair is closed for renovation. The closest all night super-market is Pick and Save.
MARY. That's way across town.
PAUL. I don't mind. We're all out of capers anyway. Will you be all right here alone?
MARY. Sure, Raoul will be right downstairs. Oh, and Paul, would you pick up a new frying pan? I hate cooking in the same one we use for bopping.
PAUL. (*Exits. HE stops at the door.*) Sure, honey. Coming, Raoul?
RAOUL. I'm coming, I'm coming. Later, Chiquita.

(RAOUL reluctantly leaves with PAUL. MARY crosses

in front of the dead body and GINGER'S hand grabs her ankle. SHE screams.)

GINGER. So, you thought you could break up the act as easy as that, did you?
MARY. Listen, Ginger, I think you better let go of me and get out of here before my husband gets back ...
GINGER. I'm afraid you've got another thing coming, Fred dear.

[Music Cue #20: MOMMA SAID - Reprise]

MOTHER SAID THAT GIRLS WHO DANCE
WERE BITCHES, WHICH IS
GOOD ADVICE THAT I SHOULD
NEVER IGNORE
YOU KNOW WHAT BAD GIRLS GET?
THE ONES WHO ARE SNITCHES?
STITCHES!
IF THERE'S A CHANCE THAT YOU WILL TELL
MOMMY WOULD SURELY GIVE ME HELL
BETTER NOT SCREAM, SAVE YOUR BREATH
I'M GONNA TAP-TAP-TAP-TAP-TAP-TAP
TAP YOU TO DEATH!

(RAOUL enters and sees MARY and GINGER struggling on the floor. RAOUL grabs the frying pan and finishes Ginger off with a triple bop. GINGER, now really dead, collapses in a heap behind the couch. MARY, deeply shaken, lies quivering on the sofa. RAOUL goes through Ginger's wallet and takes out an enormous sheaf of bills. HE whistles.)

RAOUL. Hey, Chiquita, that was a close one, eh? But, hey, look at this!
MARY. What ... how much?
RAOUL. (*Gets up and crosses to Mary on the sofa.*) A lot, Chiquita. Mucho dinero! (*HE lets the bills flutter*

down on her.) There, doesn't that feel better? Don't you feel better now?

MARY. I ... I feel so warm ...

RAOUL. (*Caresses her.*) Forget warm, Baby, you're HOT! Your blood has fire in it! You make my heart beat like a conga. You make my ...

MARY. Raoul, you shouldn't say those things, you mustn't touch me like that. Ever again! You *mustn't* ...

[Music Cue #21: LOVERS IN LOVE]

(MUSIC starts.)

RAOUL.
THE PAST FEW WEEKS THAT WE BEEN SHARIN'
THE SEXY CLOTHES THAT YOU BEEN WEARIN'
HAVE PUT A NOTION IN MY HEAD
I BET YOU'RE FABULOUS IN BED

YOU FILL MY HEART WITH DEEP DESIRE
ALONE YOU'VE SET MY LOINS ON FIRE
JUST LIKE CASANOVA SAID
WITHOUT A BOYFRIEND YOU ARE DEAD!

LOVERS IN LOVE
THAT'S WHAT WE OUGHT TO BE
LET'S YOU AND ME MAKE WE

LOVERS IN LOVE
TIED IN A LOVER'S KNOT
SEARCHING FOR YOUR "G" SPOT

LOVERS IN LOVE
WITH NOTHING BUT LOVE ON OUR MINDS
WHEN PUSH COMES TO SHOVE
LET'S GET OFF OUR BEHINDS

LOVERS IN LOVE

OUR BODIES JOINED AS ONE
HOT LIKE THE NOON DAY SUN
WE COULD HAVE TONS OF FUN
WHEN WE ARE LOVERS IN LOVE

NO OTHER CHICK THAT I COULD PICK
CLICKS INTO MY LIBIDO
YOUR SEXY FROCK KNOCKS OFF MY JOCK
WITH THE FORCE OF A TORPEDO
   MARY. Holy Toledo!
I CAN HARDLY KEEP MYSELF FROM FAINTING
YOU'RE A MATADOR FROM A VELVET PAINTING
I NEVER FELT THIS WAY BEFORE
MY CURIOSITY WANTS MORE

LOVERS IN LOVE
I FEEL A SUDDEN RUSH
EVEN MY KNEECAPS BLUSH

LOVERS IN LOVE
IS THIS MY DESTINY
WILL LUST GET THE BEST OF ME
RAOUL TAKE THE REST OF ME —

(THEY dance.)

   MARY and RAOUL.
SO WE CAN BE
   RAOUL.
LOVERS IN LOVE
   MARY.
LOVERS IN LOVE
   MARY and RAOUL.
LOVERS IN ...

(RAOUL dives onto the sofa with MARY. BLACKOUT.
The MUSIC swells with sexual excitement and then
subsides. In the DARKNESS we see a CIGARETTE

being lit.)

MARY. That was fantastic.

(LIGHTS up slowly.)

RAOUL. And it gets better, you know.
MARY. I feel so ... so ...
RAOUL. Yeah, I know what you mean.
MARY. But what we did is wrong. Shhh ... shhh. What's that?

(FOOTSTEPS and jingling KEYS are heard out in the hall.)

RAOUL. Quiet.
PAUL. *(Offstage.)* Mary, honey, can you get the door? My arms are loaded with packages. (*HE rings the bell.*)
MARY. Oh no, it's Paul. Quick get dressed.
PAUL. Mary, Mary ...
MARY. *(To Paul.)* Coming ... I'll be right there, sweetheart.
PAUL. *(Offstage.)* Hurry, my arms are breaking.
MARY. Hurry, Raoul.
RAOUL. Relax, baby, relax.

(RAOUL pulls his pants on as MARY opens the door.)

PAUL. *(Entering)* I guess I got carried ... *(Noticing Raoul.)* what's he doing here? What's going on?
MARY. *(Defensively.)* What's going on? Raoul just saved my life, that's all.
RAOUL. It was nada.
PAUL. *(Spills some of the groceries.)* What do you mean?
MARY. You didn't bop Ginger properly and if Raoul hadn't come back ...

PAUL. Why did you come back?

RAOUL. I came back to ... borrow ... uh ...

MARY. ...Tabasco... a cup of Tabasco.

RAOUL. Oh yeah, Tabasco. Listen, I got to split. Everybody's got to sleep sometime. Why don't you come to the club tomorrow night? I'm breaking in a new number.

MARY. That sounds like fun. Paul, what do you think?

PAUL. (*Brushing him off.*) Thanks, Raoul, We'll see how we feel tomorrow. But don't count on me.

RAOUL. O.K. then, see you tomorrow night Cruel Carla!

MARY. Vaya con Dios!

(RAOUL exits.)

PAUL. Vaya con Dios? Is he teaching you Spanish now?

MARY. Oh, Paul, everybody knows what "vaya con Dios" means! I'm exhausted. Shall we turn in?

PAUL. You go ahead. I'll clean up here and join you in a minute.

MARY. O.K. honey. Don't be long.

(MARY exits. PAUL starts to pick up the spilled groceries from the floor. HE reaches under the sofa and pulls out a pair of men's briefs. There is something printed on them.)

PAUL. (*Reading.*) Oh, no. Casa del whopper.

[Music Cue #22: MARY]

I SIT HERE ALL ALONE
MY WORLD HAS COME APART
EVEN THOUGH MY BILLS ARE PAID
WHAT GOOD IS ALL THIS CASH

WHEN I'VE A BROKEN HEART
I FEAR MY MARY LOVE HAS STRAYED

MY SWEET MARY, I LOVE YOU SO
I COULD NOT BEAR IT IF YOU SHOULD GO
OH, MARY, MY MUTTON CHOP
WERE YOU TO LEAVE ME, MY HEART WOULD
    STOP

I'LL BUY A SINGLE ROSE AND HOPE IT'S NOT
    TOO LATE
TO BEG MY MARY LOVE TO STAY
MAYBE I SHOULD TRY TO LOSE A LITTLE
    WEIGHT
PERHAPS I'LL WEAR A SMALL TOUPEE

MY SWEET MARY, I LOVE YOU SO
I COULD NOT BEAR IT, IF YOU SHOULD GO
OH, MARY, MY PECAN PIE
TO LIVE WITHOUT YOU, I'D RATHER DIE

PAUL. (*Writes Mary a note.*) Dear Mary, When I think that it may be over, all I want to do is die. The thought that I'll never again share another bottle of '55 Chateau Margaux with you fills my heart with pain. I love you Mary and I always will. But if you decide to go on and stir the soup without me, I guess I'll just have to spend the rest of my life at a table for one. I hope you'll be happy. Love, Paul Bland.
(*Sings.*)
MY SWEET MARY, MY CREME BRULEE
HOW CAN I KEEP YOU, I'LL FIND A WAY
WHEN ALL IS SAID AND DONE
MARY, YOU'RE THE ONE
MARY, YOU'RE THE ONE FOR ME

I LOVE YOU MORE THAN CAKE
IT'S LUCKY I DON'T BAKE
FOR WHAT WOULD CAKE WITHOUT YOU BE?

OH, MARY, PLEASE DON'T LEAVE ME

(PAUL crumples the note HE has written and exits.)

Scene 5

The CHORUS of VICTIMS cross the stage and sing.

[Music Cue #23: VICTIM UPDATE #4]

CHORUS OF VICTIMS.
NOW MARY AND PAUL
HAVE RUN INTO A SNAG
HE'LL LOSE HIS MIND
IF SHE PACKS HER BAG

WITH RAOUL ON TOP
THE WHOLE THING'S A MESS
BETTING ODDS ARE EVEN
'CAUSE IT'S ANYONE'S GUESS

IT'S MARY AND PAUL
WITH NO UPPER HAND
IT'S MARY AND PAUL AND ...

Scene 6

*The scene shifts to Yolanda's. Downstage left is a coat
   check. MARY sits alone at a ringside table stage right.
   Enter YOLANDA, her first word ["and'] overlaps with
   the last word of the chorus above.*

YOLANDA. ... And now, Raoul y las Raoulettes!!

(RAOUL and the RAOULETTES enter.)

[Music Cue #24: EATING RAOUL]

RAOUL.
YOU AND I, TOGETHER WE'LL BE FLYING HIGH
WAIT YOU'LL SEE, THEY'RE GONNA MAKE A
    STAR OF ME

THE PEOPLE WILL SCREAM
AND THE CRITICS WILL DROOL
THEY'LL BE WALKING, TALKING, BREATHING
SLEEPING, EATING RAOUL

LITTLE OLD LADIES
THE KIDS IN SCHOOL
THEY'LL BE WALKING, TALKING, BREATHING
SLEEPING, EATING RAOUL
STICK WITH ME BABY
DON'T YOU BE A FOOL
YOU'LL BE WALKING, TALKING, BREATHING
SLEEPING, EATING RAOUL

YOU AND I, WE'LL WRITE OUR NAMES ACROSS
    THE SKY
WAIT YOU'LL SEE, YOU'LL HAVE DIAMONDS
AND FAST CARS AND ME

(RAOUL jumps off stage towards Mary.)

THE PEOPLE WILL SCREAM
AND THE CRITICS WILL DROOL
THEY'LL BE WALKING, TALKING, BREATHING
SLEEPING, EATING RAOUL
PREACHERS, NUNS, RABBIS IN SHUL
THEY'LL BE WALKING, TALKING, BREATHING
SLEEPING, EATING RAOUL
STICK WITH ME BABY

DON'T YOU BE A FOOL
YOU'LL BE WALKING, TALKING, BREATHING
SLEEPING, EATING RAOUL

(To Mary.)

BABY, BABY, BABY, BABY PLEASE SAY YES
I'LL BUY YOU A FUR AND A RED SILK DRESS
MAYBE, MAYBE, MAYBE YOU'D BE LESS
    UPTIGHT
IF YOU CAME HOME TO ME EVERY NIGHT
    RAOUL and RAOULETTES.
THE PEOPLE WILL SCREAM
AND THE CRITICS WILL DROOL
THEY'LL BE WALKING, TALKING, BREATHING
SLEEPING, EATING RAOUL

A MAN ON THE STREET
A TURK IN ISTANBUL
THEY'LL BE WALKING, TALKING, BREATHING
SLEEPING, EATING RAOUL

STICK WITH ME BABY
DON'T YOU BE A FOOL
    RAOUL.
YOU'RE GONNA SEE THAT EVERY SINGLE
    MOLECULE
    RAOUL and RAOULETTES.
IS WALKING, TALKING
BREATHING, SEETHING
SLEEPING, WEEPING
BEATING, EATING RAOUL

EATING RAOUL!

(RAOUL takes his bow to much applause from MARY
    and exits to change. YOLANDA appears downstage
    left at the coat check as PAUL enters wearing a toupee

and carrying a single red rose.)

YOLANDA. Check your hat?
PAUL. I'm not wearing a hat. I wonder if you could help me. I'm looking for my wife.
YOLANDA. Only gringo chick I see tonight is Raoul's new girlfriend.
PAUL. (*Angrily.*) Where can I find Raoul?
YOLANDA. In his dressing room.
PAUL. And where is that?
YOLANDA. The kitchen.
PAUL. Gracias.

(PAUL sneaks up to the kitchen to eavesdrop. We can see RAOUL talking to PACO.)

PACO. What you got for me?
RAOUL. I got a Ford Fairlane, two Mercedes and a Cadillac. I'm thinking of keeping the Caddie for myself.
PAUL. (*Snapping his fingers.*) The cars!!!
RAOUL. I'm gonna need a new car to go with my new chick. Classy, huh?
PACO. Class, yeah, real class.
RAOUL. I just got to bump off her fat jerk of a husband and then we're off to Detroit where Raoul is gonna be the biggest thing since Tito Puente. Listen Paco, I got to get ready.
PACO. Ciao.

(PACO exits not seeing PAUL, who is standing there in horror. RAOUL goes to his mirror to dress and primp for his show.)

[Music Cue #25: TRIO]

RAOUL.
MIRA, MIRA, MIRA
ON THE WALL

LATINOS ARE THE HOTTEST LOVERS
OF THEM ALL

SUAVE, DEBONAIR,
RICARDO MONTALBAN TAN
YOU'VE GOT TO GET YOURSELF
A MUCHO MACHO MAN
   PAUL.
WHAT A CROOK
WHAT A BUM
WE WERE HAD
I FEEL SO DUMB
I'VE GOT TO STOP HIM
   RAOUL.
HOT LATINOS
   PAUL.
I'VE GOT TO STOP HIM
   RAOUL.
IN TIGHT BLACK CHINOS
   PAUL.
I'VE BEEN A FOOL
AND A JERK
HE MADE THE MONEY
WE DID THE WORK
I'VE GOT TO STOP HIM

THE GOOD FOR NOTHING WANTS TO TAKE MY
   LIFE
HE ROBS US BLIND, HE'S STEALING MY WIFE
HE STANDS FOR ALL I HAVE LEARNED TO
   ABHOR
I CAN'T TAKE IT ANYMORE
   RAOUL.
CARUMBA!
   PAUL.
I'M A MAN
NOT A MOUSE
TIME TO DUMP

THE DIRTY LOUSE
I'VE GOT TO STOP HIM
I'VE GOT TO STOP HIM
YES I DO
THIS PARTNERSHIP IS THROUGH
    RAOUL.
YOU'LL FIND THAT LATIN LOVERS TRULY ARE
    THE BEST
GO FIND A MUCHO MACHO MAN AND PUT HIM
    TO THE TEST
YOU'LL FIND THE HOT LATINO IS THE LOVER
    WHO IS BLESSED
PROOF IS IN THE PUDDING, JUST GET ONE OF
    US UNDRESSED

(The LIGHTS come up on MARY who is still sitting at
her table downstage right.)

    MARY.
I FEEL CHEAP
I FEEL USED
MY HEAD IS SPINNING
I'M SO CONFUSED
    RAOUL.
FERNANDO LAMAS
    MARY.
I THINK I LIKE IT
    RAOUL.
IN PAJAMAS
    MARY.
I THINK I LIKE IT
MOTHER SAID SEX WAS DIRTY
MOTHER'S DEAD, I'M OVER THIRTY
I THINK I LIKE IT

WHO'D HAVE THOUGHT THAT LITTLE MARY
    BLAND
COULD MELT IN THE PALM OF A LATIN LOVER'S

HAND
WHO'D HAVE GUESSED THAT THIS PROPER
   MRS. PRIM
COULD DO WHAT I DID WITH HIM
   RAOUL.
OH! HO!
   PAUL.
I'LL BE STRONG
   MARY.
ONE MORE TIME
   PAUL.
I'LL BE BRAVE
   MARY.
THEN WE'RE THROUGH
   PAUL.
I'LL SEND THAT SNAKE
   MARY.
ON SECOND THOUGHT
   PAUL.
BACK TO HIS CAVE
   MARY.
I'LL MAKE IT TWO
   PAUL.
I'VE GOT TO STOP HIM
   MARY.
I THINK I LIKE IT
   PAUL.
I'VE GOT TO STOP HIM
   MARY.
I THINK I LIKE IT
   PAUL.
YES, I DO!
   MARY.
YES, IT'S TRUE
   PAUL.
YES, I DO!
AND PERHAPS I'LL BOP HIM TOO

PAUL, MARY, RAOUL.
(Lyrics as above except for Raoul's which follow.)
  RAOUL.
NOBODY CAN LOVE YOU LIKE A HOT LATINO
  CAN
YOU GOT TO FIND YOURSELF A MUCHO MACHO
  MAN
SUAVE DEBONAIR, RICARDO MONTALBAN TAN
YOU GOT TO FIND YOURSELF A MUCHO MACHO
  MAN

HOT LIKE A JALAPENA
LISTEN, NINA
TIGHT BLACK CHINOS,
HOT LATINOS

NOBODY CAN LOVE YOU LIKE A HOT LATINO
  CAN
YOU GOT TO FIND YOURSELF A MUCHO MACHO
  MAN

(PAUL throws the toupee and rose to the ground and storms out of the club.)

BLACKOUT

Scene 7

Yolanda's, after hours. As the LIGHTS come up, MARY and RAOUL are discovered on the stage. THEY have just made love.

RAOUL. Baby, that's the most fun I had since I was sixteen!
MARY. Raoul, as much as I've enjoyed our time together, this has to be our last.

RAOUL. Very funny, Chiquita.

MARY. No, I'm serious. Paul and I will have our restaurant soon and, well, I don't want anything to jeopardize our future.

RAOUL. You are crazy! What kind of future can you have with a slob like him? You need a real man.

MARY. Paul's warm and loyal and my best friend.

RAOUL. I'll buy you a dog.

MARY. But, but ...

RAOUL. Just think of our life together. You could make me very happy. Wouldn't you like that?

[Music Cue #26: EATING RAOUL - Reprise]

RAOUL.
BABY, BABY, BABY, BABY PLEASE SAY YES
I'LL BUY YOU A FUR AND A RED SILK DRESS
MAYBE, MAYBE, MAYBE YOU'D BE LESS
   UPTIGHT
IF YOU CAME HOME TO ME EVERY NIGHT
WALKING, TALKING, BREATHING, SEETHING,
SLEEPING, WEEPING, BEATING,
EATING RA ...

(SHE pulls him down into an embrace.)

BLACKOUT

Scene 8

The Bland's apartment. PAUL is sitting in the DARK on the couch. MARY enters the apartment and switches on the LIGHTS, discovering Paul.

MARY. Paul, why are you sitting in the dark?
PAUL. The cars!

MARY. What are you talking about?

PAUL. Raoul. That's where he gets all that money! He hunts for the keys in our clients pockets and then sells their cars.

MARY. If you're going to start on Raoul again, it will have to wait till morning. I'm exhausted.

PAUL. I bet!

MARY. Oh, Paul!

PAUL. Mary, you don't know what he's planning.

MARY. You're just being paranoid. I'm going to bed.

PAUL. No you're not. Donna called. She's invited us to an all night bash in Beverly Hills.

MARY. Paul, I can't. Not tonight ...

PAUL. I spoke to James. We have to get the rest of the money for the down payment by tomorrow night. Donna says this party will be full of high rollers. This is our last chance for happiness.

MARY. But it's so late, what if we can't find Raoul...

PAUL. We're going without Raoul. The partnership is finished.

MARY. But ...

PAUL. No buts, Mary. We're going and we're going alone. Now go change.

MARY. All right, Paul. But I do feel funny about not telling Raoul. After all, he is our friend. (*SHE exits to the bedroom to change.*)

PAUL. (*In a total rage.*) Our friend?!?!?! He seduces my wife, he plots to kill me and he's robbing us blind. I guess you could call that a friend.

[Music Cue #27: I'M GONNA STOP HIM]

(*HE sings*)

I'M A MAN, NOT A MOUSE
IT'S TIME TO DUMP THE DIRTY LOUSE

I'VE GOT TO STOP HIM
I'VE GOT TO STOP HIM
YES I DO
AND PERHAPS I'LL BOP HIM TOO!!!!!

BLACKOUT

Scene 9

The patio of a Beverly Hills mansion. There is a barbecue, a hot tub and everything you would expect. DONNA is leading the CHORUS of SWINGERS.

[Music Cue #27a: SWING, SWING, SWING - Reprise]

DONNA and SWINGERS.
WE'RE KISSIN', WE'RE HUGGIN'
WE'RE DRINKIN', WE'RE DRUGGIN'
WE'RE CRUISIN', WE'RE CHOOSIN'
EVERYONE HERE WANTS TO SWING
WE'RE RANTIN', WE'RE RAVIN'
WE'RE MASTER-AND-SLAVIN'
WE'RE BOOZIN', WE'RE BRUISIN'
EVERYONE HERE WANTS TO SWING
DONNA.
WE'RE IN BEVERLY HILLS WHERE WE'RE
    POPPIN' PILLS
AND THE CHEAPEST THRILLS COST A LOT
WE'RE MAKIN' DATES, SHARIN' MATES
SNORTIN' COKE, SMOKIN' POT
DONNA and SWINGERS.
ALL OF US LIVE FOR JUST ONE THING
WE WANT TO SWING, SWING, SWING!

(As the MUSIC continues PAUL and MARY enter and are greeted by DONNA, in her full S&M regalia.)

DONNA. The Blands! I was just about to give up on you two.

MARY. Hi, Donna.

PAUL. You look ... lovely.

DONNA. Come on in.

DONNA and SWINGERS.
WE'RE CAMPIN', WE'RE VAMPIN'
THE LADIES ARE TRAMPIN'
WE'RE SWITCHIN', WE'RE SWAPPIN'
OUR UNDIES ARE DROPPIN'
WE'RE SMOOCHIN', WE'RE STRIPPIN'
WE'RE ALL SKINNY DIPPIN'
WE'RE HAVING ONE HELL OF A FLING
WE'RE PINCHIN', WE'RE PETTIN'
IN CASE YOU'RE FORGETTIN'
SUMMER, FALL, WINTER AND SPRING
EVERYONE HERE WANTS TO SWING

(As the MUSIC continues Paul and Mary are approached by MR. LEECH who sings.)

MR. LEECH.
WELL, MRS. BLAND, I COULD FLIP!
THOUGHT YOU WERE A STUCK-UP DRIP
COULD THIS BE YOUR LUCKY SPOUSE
WELCOME TO MY HUMBLE HOUSE
GET A DRINK, GRAB SOME GRUB
SEE YOU LATER IN THE TUB

(LEECH exits. DONNA approaches Paul and Mary, leading a GUEST on a leash.)

DONNA. Well, I've found my date for the evening.

GUEST. Beat me, Donna. Whip me, make me write bad checks!

DONNA. *(Places her spiked heel in his neck.)* Wait till I get you home, you little cockroach.

(The GUEST squeals with pleasure.)

DONNA. *(To Paul and Mary.)* This party is full of jerks, but some of them are really rich. Happy hunting! *(To the Guest.)* You follow me. I'm in the blue Chevy.

(DONNA exits the party with GUEST on a leash.)

MARY. Paul, let's get out of here. These people are just too tacky! It's degrading, it's exhausting, and I'm going home.

PAUL. We can't just throw away all our months of hard work! Come on, we're almost home free. Just a few more clients and we'll have our country kitchen ...

(The hot tub is now full of SWINGERS, led by MR. LEECH.)

LEECH.
EVERYONE INTO THE TUB
LEECH and SWINGERS.
WE'RE PLEASIN', WE'RE THANKIN'
WE'RE GETTIN' A SPANKIN'
WE'RE TYIN', WE'RE ROPIN'
WE'RE INTO GROUP GROPIN'
WE'RE BITIN', WE'RE BAITIN'
WE'RE ALL FORNICATIN'
EVERYONE'S DOIN' HIS THING

WE'RE PIMPIN', WE'RE PEEPIN'
TOGETHER WE'RE SLEEPIN'
WHO KNOWS WHAT THE MORNING WILL BRING
EVERYONE HERE WANTS TO SWING
LEECH.
COOL IT BLAND WHAT'S THE RUB
I SAID EVERYONE INTO THE TUB
PAUL. Shut up!

LEECH. (*Sings.*)
YOUR PRETTY WIFE NEEDS A BIG WET KISS
WE WANT TO SWING, SWING, SWING
　MARY. Mind your own business!
　LEECH and SWINGERS. (*Sing.*)
WE WANT TO SWING, SWING, SWING
　PAUL. Butt out, I'm warning you.
　LEECH and SWINGERS. (*Sing.*)
WE WANT TO SWING, SWING, SWING
　PAUL. Well, swing on this!

*(Livid with rage, HE picks up one of the electrical heaters
　and heaves it into the hot tub. There is a flash of
　LIGHT and a cry of pleasure from the SWINGERS as
　THEY die.)*

Scene 10

*Paul and Mary's living room later that night. PAUL is
　making a telephone call as MARY sorts through a pile
　of expensive clothing.*

　PAUL. Hello, Aristocrat Used Cars? Do you guys
have one of those double-decker auto transport trailers?
You do? Good. Well, send it over to 7860 Fareholm
Drive as quick as you can. We've got a bonanza for you.

*(As HE hangs up, HE smiles at MARY, who has been
　counting money.)*

　MARY. Three thousand seven hundred and forty-two
dollars so far. And I just started!
　PAUL. I bet there's another twenty thousand in cars.
　MARY. I still feel funny about not calling Raoul.
　PAUL. After last night, we won't ever need Raoul
again. I won't miss him. Will you?

(PAUL exits into the bedroom but immediately reappears walking backwards with his arms raised. RAOUL follows him into the living room holding a gun.)

RAOUL. Don't worry Chiquita! The time has come to liberate you.

PAUL. Listen, Raoul ...

RAOUL. Shut up! You going to dump me, huh? Well, Mary and me are going to dump you! Nobody's going to take this beautiful, sexy chick and make her sweat in some stinking country kitchen!

MARY. Raoul ...

RAOUL. Keep cool, baby. You and me're going to Detroit where Raoul will be the biggest thing since Louis Prima. But first I got a little business to take care of. Chiquita, go bring me that frying pan.

MARY. Raoul ...

(The LIGHTS fade as RAOUL and PAUL fall behind the couch, struggling over the gun. MARY is isolated in a SPOTLIGHT.)

[Music Cue #28: ONE LAST BOP]

MARY.
I'M FACE TO FACE
WITH A CRITICAL DECISION
STANDING AT THE CROSSROADS OF MY LIFE
I MUST STAY CALM
LETTING NOTHING BLUR MY VISION
AM I A LATIN'S LOVER OR A FAITHFUL WIFE

IT COULD NOT LAST
IT WAS ME WHO I WAS FOOLIN'
THE TIME HAS COME
I'VE GOT TO CHOOSE MY MAN
AM I GONNA BOP PAUL

OR DO I DO RAOUL IN?
MY DESTINY LIES IN THIS FRYING PAN

ONE BOP, ONE LAST BOP
THIS DOUBLE LIFE I'M LEADING
WILL COME TO A STOP
ONE BOP, ONE BOP IT'S OVER

ONE BOP, ONE LAST BOP
I CAN THROW AWAY THE HANDCUFFS
AND THE RIDING CROP
ONE BOP, ONE BOP IT'S OVER

I MAY NEVER HAVE SEX AGAIN
IF I BOP MY SEXY MEXICAN

I NEVER THOUGHT I WOULD END UP IN THIS
    PICKLE
THINGS HAVE NOT TURNED OUT THE WAY I
    PLANNED
YET HERE I AM, FUNNY FATE IS FICKLE
I HOLD THE FUTURE RIGHT HERE IN MY HAND

ONE BOP, ONE LAST BOP
THIS DOUBLE LIFE I'M LEADING
WILL COME TO A STOP
ONE BOP, ONE BOP IT'S OVER

ONE BOP, ONE LAST BOP
IT LOOKS LIKE WE'RE GONNA HAVE TO
CLOSE UP SHOP
ONE BOP, ONE BOP

ONE LAST BOP
ONE LAST BOP
ONE LAST BOP

[Music Cue #28a: AFTER BOP]

(MARY wields her frying pan and we hear the one last bop. BONK! We do not see which one she hits.)

Scene 1

The LIGHTS slowly fade up. MARY and JAMES are seated on the couch, laughing. THEY have champagne glasses.

MARY. James, you're so funny.
JAMES. Such a wonderful lunch to celebrate such a wonderful occasion!
MARY. It was nothing really. We just improvised with what we had lying around the house.

(PAUL enters from the kitchen with a large tureen.)

JAMES. You know, it's times like these, when I see two wonderful people like yourselves get the house of your dreams, that my job becomes more than just something to do from nine to five. Bravo!
PAUL. That's very kind of you, James. *(PAUL places the tureen on the table and takes his seat.)*
JAMES. No, I mean it! It's great to see decent people make it who haven't clawed their way to get there!
MARY. That's a real compliment, especially coming from a real estate agent.
PAUL. *(Opens the lid of the tureen and steam pours out.)* More stew?
JAMES. *(Helping himself.)* It's absolutely sensational. I trust it's going to be a permanent item on your menu. It's French, isn't it?
MARY. Actually, it's Mexican.
JAMES. The meat is so tender!
MARY. *(Fondly.)* Yes, I know ...

PAUL. (*In triumph.*) It's amazing what you can do with a cheap piece of meat, if you know how to treat it.

(*JAMES takes a bite of stew. THEY raise their glasses of champagne in a toast.*)

PAUL. A toast ... to absent friends. Vaya con dios!
MARY and JAMES. Vaya con dios!

(*THEY clink their glasses as the CHORUS of VICTIMS crosses the stage and sings.*
A curtain closes and as the CHORUS sings the finale, the curtain opens revealing MARY and PAUL in a double bed.)

[Music Cue #29: FINALE]

CHORUS.
NOW MARY AND PAUL
WE'RE SURE YOU CAN GUESS
HAVE OPENED UP A RESTAURANT
A MAJOR SUCCESS

YOU'VE GOT TO ADMIT
THEY HAD COURAGE AND NERVE
AND NO ONE GOT A SINGLE THING
THEY DIDN'T DESERVE

AND ON THE ANNIVERSARY
OF THE DAY THEY WERE WED,
THEY WENT OUT AND BOUGHT THEMSELVES
A BIG DOUBLE BED

SO MARY AND PAUL
WITH THEIR LITTLE SCHEME
BOUGHT THEMSELVES A PIECE
OF THE AMERICAN DREAM

MARY AND PAUL
DID WHAT THEY HAD TO DO
MARY AND PAUL
THEIR STORY IS TRUE
MARY AND PAUL
LET'S GIVE 'EM A HAND
MARY AND PAUL
MARY AND PAUL
MARY AND PAUL ... BLAND

BLACKOUT

CURTAIN

Note On Alternate Scene

During the run of the New York production of *Eating Raoul* it became necessary, due to technical difficulties, to abandon Scene 9 in Act II, the final swinger party with its electricution effect. Scenes 8 and 10 were combined in the version which follows. This foreshortened version of the play may be used at the director's discretion.

ALTERNATE SCENE

The Bland's apartment. PAUL is sitting in the dark on the couch. MARY enters, switches on the lights, discovers Paul.

MARY. Paul, why are you sitting in the dark?
PAUL. The cars!
MARY. What are you talking about?
PAUL. Raoul. That's where he gets all that money! He hunts for the keys in our clients pockets and then sells their cars.
MARY. If you're going to start on Raoul again, it will have to wait till morning. I'm exhausted.
PAUL. I bet!
MARY. Oh, Paul!
PAUL. Donna called. She's invited us to an all night bash in Beverly Hills
MARY. Paul, I can't. Not tonight ...
PAUL. And I spoke to James. We have to get the rest of the money for the down payment by tomorrow night. Donna says this party will be full of high rollers. This is our last chance for happiness.
MARY. But it's so late, what if we can't find Raoul.
PAUL. We're going without Raoul. The partnership is finished.
MARY. But ...
PAUL. No buts, Mary. We're going and we're going alone. (*Suddenly forceful.*) Now go change!

MARY. All right, Paul. Whatever you say. (*SHE exits to the bedroom to change.*)

[Music Cue #27: I'M GONNA STOP HIM]

PAUL.
I'M A MAN, NOT A MOUSE
IT'S TIME TO DUMP THE DIRTY LOUSE
I'VE GOT TO STOP HIM
I'VE GOT TO STOP HIM
YES I DO...

(*The DOORBELL rings. PAUL answers it. RAOUL enters with a gun aimed at Paul.*)

PAUL. Listen, Raoul ...
RAOUL. Shut up! You going to dump me, huh? Well, Mary and me are going to dump you! Nobody's going to take this beautiful, sexy chick and make her sweat in some stinking country kitchen! We're gonna expand this business. Bring in some real sexy, younger girls to dress up instead of my wife who'll be too busy having my kids!

(*MARY enters dressed in a slip and boots, dressed for the party.*)

MARY. Raoul!
RAOUL. Don't worry Chiquita! The time has come to liberate you.
MARY. Raoul ...
RAOUL. Keep cool, Baby, I got twenty "G's" right here.
PAUL. That's our money, the money you stole from us!
RAOUL. In a minute Mary and me will be off to Detroit where Raoul will be the biggest thing since Tito Puente. Chiquita, go bring me that frying pan.

(The LIGHTS fade as RAOUL and PAUL fall behind the couch, fighting for the gun. MARY is isolated in a SPOTLIGHT.)

[Music Cue #28: ONE LAST BOP]

MARY.
I'M FACE TO FACE
WITH A CRITICAL DECISION
STANDING AT THE CROSSROADS OF MY LIFE
I MUST STAY CALM
LETTING NOTHING BLUR MY VISION
AM I A LATIN'S LOVER OR A FAITHFUL WIFE

IT COULD NOT LAST
IT WAS ME WHO I WAS FOOLIN'
THE TIME HAS COME
I'VE GOT TO CHOOSE MY MAN
AM I GONNA BOP PAUL
OR DO I DO RAOUL IN?
MY DESTINY LIES IN THIS FRYING PAN

ONE BOP, ONE LAST BOP
THIS DOUBLE LIFE I'M LEADING
WILL COME TO A STOP
ONE BOP, ONE BOP IT'S OVER

ONE BOP, ONE LAST BOP
I CAN THROW AWAY THE HANDCUFFS
AND THE RIDING CROP
ONE BOP, ONE BOP IT'S OVER

I MAY NEVER HAVE SEX AGAIN
IF I BOP THAT SEXY MEXICAN

I NEVER THOUGHT I WOULD END UP IN THIS
   PICKLE

THINGS HAVE NOT TURNED OUT THE WAY I
    PLANNED
YET HERE I AM, FUNNY FATE IS FICKLE
I HOLD THE FUTURE RIGHT HERE IN MY HAND

ONE BOP, ONE LAST BOP
THIS DOUBLE LIFE I'M LEADING
WILL COME TO A STOP
ONE BOP, ONE BOP IT'S OVER

ONE BOP, ONE LAST BOP
IT LOOKS LIKE WE'RE GONNA HAVE TO
CLOSE UP SHOP
ONE BOP, ONE BOP
ONE LAST BOP
ONE LAST BOP
ONE LAST BOP

*(As the LIGHTS fade, MARY wields her frying pan
    behind the couch and we hear the one last BONK! We
    do not see which one she hits.)*

BLACKOUT

COSTUME PLOT
ACT I

MARY
1. Nightgown and bathrobe
2. Nurse's uniform
3. S&M outfit
4. S&M nun's wimple
5. Cheerleader skirt and sweater
6. Chef's hat and apron
PAUL
1. Pajamas and bathrobe
2. Jacket, shirt, tie and trousers
3. S&M outfit,Black shirt, pants and mask
4. Priest's collar
5. Chef's hat
RAOUL
1. Tee shirt and jeans
CHORUS MALE #1
1. Swinger
2. Doctor's uniform
3. S&M face mask, lycra bikini and boots
4. Chicken suit
5. Snow man
6. loud blazer and tie
CHORUS MALE #2
1. Swinger
2. Liquor shop owner
3. S&M face mask, lycra bikini and boots
4. Nehru suit
4. Fat suit
CHORUS MALE #3
1. Swinger
2. Business suit
3. Parochial school uniform
CHORUS FEMALE #1
1. Swinger
2. Metermaid

3. S&M backup singer, body stocking with strategic black bars
4. Sexy hot pants and top
CHORUS FEMALE #2
1. Swinger
2..S&M backup singer, body stocking with strategic black bars
3. Sexy hot pants and top
CHORUS FEMALE #3
1. Swinger
2. Dominatrix
3. Basketball player
4. Donna at home, white shirt, jeans and sneakers

ACT TWO

MARY
1. Daytime dress
2. Coat, purse and hat
3. Ginger Rogers ballgown and blonde wig
4. Dress, coat, hat.
5. Pool outfit
6. Slip
7. Penoir
PAUL
1. Shirt and tie, jacket and slacks
2. White tie and tails
3. Cabana outfit
4. Smoking jacket
RAOUL
1. Sexy jungle outfit
2. Sexy leather jump suit
2. White tie and tails
4. Jeans and tee shirt
CHORUS MALE #1
1. Latino band member
2. Tee shirt and jeans
4. Swinger bathing suit

CHORUS MALE #2
1. Latino band member
2.Ginger Rogers ball gown and blonde wig
3.Swinger bathing suit
CHORUS MALE #3
1. Hitler
2. Latino band member
3. Swinger bathing suit
CHORUS FEMALE #1
1. Raoulette jungle outfit
2. Raoulette go-go costume
4. Swinger bathing suit
CHORUS FEMALE #2
1. Raoulette jungle costume
2. Raoulette go-go costume
4. Swinger bathing suit
CHORUS FEMALE #3
1. Yolanda's hostess mumu
2. Donna's S&M outfit
3. Swinger bathing suit

PROPERTY PLOT
ACT I

MARY: Comb, brush, purse, dry cleaning, stack of mail, silver ruler, pom poms, basket ball hoop, letter

PAUL: Groceries, trick frying pan

DR DOBERMAN: Clipboard

MR. KRAY: Cigar, case of wine

METERMAID: Parking tickets, pen

DONNA: Whip, business card (AT HOME) baby, baby bottle, stuffed animal

MUSCLEMAN 1: Pitch pipe

MUSCLEMAN 2: Rope

JAMES: Briefcase, floor plans, snap shots

BOBBY: School bag, lunch box, money

BASKET BALL PLAYER: Basketball, money

JUNIOR: Money

CHICKEN: Bucket of Chicken Delight with attached bill

RAOUL: Flashlight ,tool belt

GLADYS: Six pack of Colt 45

INEZ: Portable radio

ACT II

MARY: 2 Purses, champagne glass, Hitler moustache, trick frying pan

PAUL: Rose, toupee, champagne glass, soup tureen, space heater, money, pads and pencils, Hitler moustache, Nazi flag, bikini briefs with writing, groceries, glitter drape

RAOUL: Comb, money, flight bag, gun, cigarette, lighter

GINGER: Money

GENERAL: Chair, box of costumes, Nazi pillows, torn drape, drinking glasses

LOCATIONS

ACT I

Mary and Paul's bedroom
The streets of L.A.
The hospital
Kray's liquor store
Bank
Hallway outside of Mary and Paul's apartment
Mary and Paul's living room
Donna's kitchen

ACT II

Yolanda's night club
Raoul's dressing room
Patio of Beverly Hills mansion (optional)

www.ingramcontent.com/pod-product-compliance
Lightning Source LLC
Chambersburg PA
CBHW070346120726
47909CB00008B/2747